All's Fairy in Love & War

by Rachel Roberts

All's Fairy in Love & War

by Rachel Roberts

New York

First Edition

ISBN 1-59315-011-3

Cover Illustration by Jim Carroll
Cover Design by Richard Aquan

With special thanks to our friends, Emily, Andie and Urvashi for their help.

Chapter 1

"Ow!"

Kara dropped her script for the school play and shook her fingers hard. Ordinarily the thirteen-year-old wasn't clumsy, but in her haste to "rise and outshine" this morning, she'd grabbed for the safety pin without looking to see that it was closed. It wasn't.

Unsurprisingly, Kara had nabbed the starring role in her school production of Shakespeare's *A Midsummer Night's Dream.* She'd play the Fairy Queen Titania, with typical grace and style—*and* a killer costume. This pink and poufy dress, to be exact.

She whipped around in front of her full-length mirror.

Whack! The costume's wide silk wings flapped open, smacking the back of her head. Okay, scratch the grace and style.

"They're still crooked!" she whined.

"Stand still, I'm not finished." The reproach came

to her telepathically, in a familiar purring voice. It was from the exquisite leopard-like cat at her side, whose whiskery mouth was clamped down on six safety pins.

"That doesn't look right, Lyra," Kara complained to her feline friend, looking over her shoulder at her reflection.

"I think I know a few things about wings," the cat replied, emerald green eyes twinkling. She wasn't kidding: She was a magical animal, a winged cat Kara had bonded with.

Ding! Kara's pink laptop, perched precariously on the edge of her canopy bed, signaled an incoming IM.

She sighed dramatically. What would her friends do without her? With one wing attached, the other half-pinned and dragging on the carpet, she grabbed the hem of her dress and strode over to her bed.

The IM-er was Molly, aka goodgollymolly:

goodgollymolly: k, u sure this green base will come off? ☹

With one hand, she tapped back a message to Molly, who was working on her makeup for her role as one of the fairies in the play.

kstar: just apply a light coat, u'r a fairy, not the hulk!

goodgollymolly: ooo I luv the glitter sprinkles, wait till u c ☺

Kara had started back toward the mirror when the pink phone on her desk began to ring. Without thinking, she hit the speaker.

"So what's the story on the cast party?" Heather was already in full-whine mode. "And these sleeves are too puffy."

"Hello? They're cap sleeves. They're supposed to be puffy," Kara reminded her friend.

Tiffany cut through the convo, reading her lines dramatically: " 'Those be rubies, fairy favors; in those freckles live their savors.' How's that?"

"No one will notice with that incredible costume," Kara assured her, inspecting her own dress. She adjusted the scoop neck on the bodice, checking that the crystal beading was threaded perfectly down the front.

Lyra nimbly nosed the wide wings in place.

La-la-la-la-la-la. Her cell phone, half-buried in her pillows, sang out. Now what?

A split second before hitting "Talk," she glanced at the Caller ID, and frowned.

"Hi, it's me," Emily said, her voice betraying a trace of anxiety. "How's the play going?"

"Fine," Kara answered. She knew she sounded curt, but Emily didn't seem to notice.

"I just called to remind you we're meeting with

Adriane at Ravenswood this weekend," Emily said, "We need something really exciting to announce the new tourist season."

Ravenswood was an animal sanctuary that she, Emily, and Adriane were in charge of. A year ago, Kara would have scoffed at such a lame idea—but a year ago, she didn't know she was a mage. And she could never share that secret with Heather, Tiffany, and Molly.

"Hey, Princess Rapunzel!" Suddenly, another voice, impatient, broke in. "How are we going to keep feeding the animals without the council's support?" It was Adriane, already channeling her inner Warrior. So early in the morning! Kara refused to respond.

"And we're swamped at Ravenswood with e-mails," Emily added. "Not to mention the mage mission of retrieving the missing power crystals."

Not trying very hard to hide her exasperation, Kara told them, "Yeah, yeah. The show's tomorrow, so you'll have to live without me until then."

"Kara, we need you!" Everyone wailed and dinged at once from the phones and the computer.

"Take a chill pill. It's under control," Kara said. Fairies, pick me up in thirty minutes." She hung up the landlines.

"Good luck with the show," Emily said.

"Thanks. Later." Kara hit the "End Call" button, tossing the cell into the pile of stuffed animals that lined her window seat. Then she stomped back to the mirror. Why did those two girls always make her feel so . . . so angry! There was more to life than using magic, even if it *was* for the cause of Ravenswood and the . . . she turned to see Lyra staring at her with her big green cat eyes.

Kara flushed. "It's not about you."

"You don't have to apologize for how you feel," the cat said, stretching on the wide rug and licking the fur on her left front leg.

"Stop being so . . . understanding!"

Her whole morning routine was being disrupted! She adjusted the sparkling tiara and brushed her long golden hair.

Adriane and Emily took to magic like ducks to water. Kara's magic only frustrated her. Sure, Kara was totally into the excitement, the thrill of using magic. But the kind of excitement she had managed to stir up was the kind that could kill a person. And who needed that kind of stress? Not me, thought Kara. All this worrying about how to use her magic was enough to bring on a stress attack—or worse, a bad complexion.

And after all she'd been through, she still couldn't understand her blazing star powers. She'd accidentally absorbed shapeshifting magic, only the ability didn't come with instructions. She had finally gotten it under control only to lose it again.

And now she was right back where she had

started. One incredibly powerful magic jewel and no idea what to do with it.

It was time to face facts: She was never going to master the magic of the unicorn jewel. It was high time to get back to what was real. In just three short weeks Kara had managed to work on all kinds of projects, including putting herself in the middle of the school play, part of Shakespeare Day at Stonehill Middle School.

But now she was beginning to feel totally swamped—being pulled from all directions. Between the mage quest, Ravenswood, the school play, and her friends, it seemed she had no time to spare.

Chill, she told herself. I'll figure this out, and *without* magic!

She looked at Lyra and reprimanded herself. Without magic, she never would have met her best friend. She thought about how many lives were at stake. After all, she, Emily, and Adriane weren't the only ones in danger. The whole reason they had gotten involved in this mess was to help the animals—Phel, Ozzie, Stormbringer, and countless others from Aldenmor and beyond. And now Storm was gone. Who knew what had happened to Phel. And the web was totally flooie. And they were the ones, no—*she* was the one—who had released all that magic from Avalon. Not Emily, not Adriane, not Ozzie, not the Fairimentals. She, *moi!* How could she be the only one to have released that m power?

Kara was overwhelmed just thinking about it. What if she was never meant to use magic? What if it was all some horrible mistake? What if she never found out what being a blazing star really meant? The thoughts made her sick to her stomach. She wanted to tell Emily and Adriane how scared she was, but she couldn't. People depended on her to be a certain way. Calm, cool, and in control. It was as though they expected her to be as flawless on the inside as she was on the outside. And who was she to let them down? Sure, the pressure to be perfect was hard to bear. But the thought of disappointing people was even harder.

If you have a test, you prepare, she thought as she slipped into the outfit's matching sparkly slippers. But how do you prepare for a fight to save the entire web of magic? Or creatures that could eat you alive and still have room for your friends?

She flopped down on the bed, yanking up her white leggings under the skirt. Then she stood in front of the mirror. "Perfect!" Kara was pleased with the full effect of the glorious costume. The pearly white wings looked especially real, sparkling like a magical butterfly.

A sudden static charge sparkled through the room. The lights dimmed, went black, and came back on.

That's odd. . . . It's not the season for a brown-out, Kara thought.

Then she noticed something *really* odd, a bright light outlining her closet door. Even with the door closed, she could see the light shimmering and swirling from inside.

Kara looked to Lyra questioningly. The cat was crouched, ready to spring, hair bristling along her neck.

Kara cocked her head. She heard sniffing and whispering—someone was in her closet!

"Eeek!" Kara leaped onto her bed.

"Where are we?" a squeaky voice asked.

"I don't know," a second voice answered gruffly.

"Well, look at the map," the high-pitched voice whispered.

"It's not on the map!"

"Lemme see that thing!"

The closet door slowly creaked open, sending bright light spiraling around Kara's room.

A long nose poked through the crack in the door, sniffing. "I smell magic!" the squeaky-voiced creature said, whiskers twitching.

"Get out there and take a look!" the other said.

"No way. *You* go!"

"No, you!"

The door burst open. A large rat and a pointy-eared goblin-like creature rolled onto the rug, tussling.

"Hey!" Kara leaped to the floor, Lyra growling at her side.

"Ahhhh!" The startled creatures jumped back, scrambling into a case of books and knocking over a shelf of fashion magazines.

"We can explain everything!" the squeaky-voiced creature said, shaking with fear. It looked like a big dog-sized rat, long nose and whiskers quivering.

"Sparky, it's her!" The other eyed Kara and her glittering outfit carefully. He looked like a boy, except he had green skin and pointy ears. He wore a leather aviator cap with goggles, black vest with lots of pockets, and red pants tucked into knee-high boots. A thick belt full of brightly colored vials wrapped around his waist.

"We're rich!" the rat thing squealed. "Oop—"

Lyra stepped in front of Kara, growling.

"Spare us, Princess." The rat quivered, eyeing the ferocious-looking cat.

"Who are you?" Kara demanded.

The strange boy bowed. "Princess, I am the great hobgoblin explorer, Musso the Magnificent, and this is my assistant mookrat magic sniffer, Sparky."

"Assistant?" The mookrat shifted beady black eyes.

"Quiet, you still get thirty percent."

"Hey!" the mookrat snarled, wiggling his long nose. "You said I could get twenty-five!"

"Fine, have it your way." He turned back to Kara. "My *associate* and I have been surfing the magic web for days. We have braved the treacherous wild magic in nothing but a bubble on this most excellent adventure to find you."

"Is that a portal in my closet?!" Kara asked, looking at the unbelievable swirling light hanging in the middle of her Capri pants. Through its center, Kara saw spirals of stars stretching across the infinite lines of the magic web.

"It's a porta-portal," Sparky said.

"What my hairy friend here is saying is that this portal is moving."

"I sniffed our way here," Sparky announced, nose wagging proudly.

"Yes, so if you are ready, Princess, we must be off before it clos-ak—" Musso reached for Kara, but was blocked by a mouthful of Lyra's razor teeth.

"What are you talking about?" Kara asked Musso.

"We were hired to find you so you can save the magic web."

Sparky looked at Musso. "How's she gonna do that?"

Musso poked Sparky on the snout. "She's the blazing star, you nosepod!"

"Ooo, blazing star!"

"I'm not going anywhere!" Kara said adamantly. "So go back wherever you came from."

"But there's major trouble," Musso cried. "Everyone needs you!"

"Take a number," Kara said, holding up her jewel. The gem suddenly erupted with diamond-bright light.

"AK!" Musso and Sparky dove out of the way as the portal pulsed wildly, drawing in the magic of the unicorn jewel.

Kara was jerked forward, her necklace biting into the back of her neck. "Ahh, Lyra! It's pulling my jewel in!"

Lyra sprang in front of Kara, pushing the girl back.

Musso and Sparky leaped, pulling Kara forward.

"Hurry, it's closing!" Musso yelled, looking anxiously as the bright portal spun in on itself.

With a fierce growl, Lyra swiped at the two intruders. They scrambled apart, trying to avoid the sharp claws.

Kara went flying forward, jewel first, into the portal. "Lyra!" she screamed.

Lyra raced into the closet and leaped, diving through the dwindling hole. The portal closed and vanished, leaving a perplexed Musso and Sparky stranded in Kara's bedroom.

Chapter 2

Kara fell like Alice down the rabbit hole, tumbling and landing in a heap.

"Lyra!" she called frantically, struggling to untangle herself from her voluminous skirt, spitting blond hair from her face.

"I am here." The cat was behind her, emerald eyes warily surveying the immediate area.

Kara followed Lyra's gaze. Golden brown trees with wide trunks soared overhead, twisting sunlight into shafts of shimmering shadows. She'd fallen into a glade in the woods. A clump of purple heather had cushioned her fall. Jasmine, peach blossoms, and clover filled her senses.

Something flew by Kara's face, accompanied by a flourish of tinkling bells.

"Hey!" Kara stammered, readjusting the straps on her fairy wings.

Luminous wide eyes looked at Kara. They were tiny figures, about the size of butterflies. Translucent wings of intricate beauty pulsed with light and formed swirling patterns in the air.

"Fairy wraiths," Lyra explained as they merrily whirled around her. *"We must be in the Fairy Realms."*

Kara stood and smoothed out the long dress, checking for stains.

"Great! No sign of a portal for weeks, and one opens in my closet!"

Catching a glint out of the corner of her eye, Kara spun around. Furry heads peeked out from behind rocks. Something that looked like a small bear with glimmering purple fur sat staring at Kara with big golden eyes. Birds of deep greens, reds, and purples fluttered above her head, chirping excitedly.

"Shoo!" Kara tried to swipe them away. "Let's just find that portal and jump back through," she said to Lyra.

"That's what I've been looking for. There's no sign of a portal anywhere around here," Lyra responded.

"Then how did we get here?"

A troop of brave squirrel-like creatures with orange tufted ears had moved toward Kara's feet. Their bushy tails swept the forest floor as they investigated the girl.

Kara looked down to see the front of her dress glowing with a brilliant hue. She fished the unicorn jewel from inside her bodice. The gem was ablaze with light.

"I'm a magical lighthouse!" Kara quickly willed her jewel to calm down.

"Scritch!!!" An adamant orange squirrel thingy demanded.

Kara sighed. Fine. "One scritch." She reached out—but the animal squealed in horror.

In a mad rush, *all* the creatures bolted, leaving Kara and Lyra alone.

"What? I took a shower." Suddenly she gasped. "Oh great, will you look at this!" Mud had stained the glittering hem of her dress where the squirrels had been.

"Ssshorrrible."

"Take it easy, Lyra," Kara said, brushing the mud away. "The dry cleaner can get it out."

"That wasn't me," the cat answered, crouching low, green eyes searching the woods.

Something moved among the trees. Hints of light sparkled from yellow eyes.

"What else am I attracting?" Kara asked, suddenly aware of how vulnerable they were in the open forest.

"Stay behind me," the cat ordered, hackles raised.

There was something in the shadows. It was as if the trees themselves had spawned horrible misshapen creatures. Their bodies were thick wood, standing on bowed legs. Thorns sprouted from thin arms ending in long, sharp fingers. Wide, flat faces rimed with thorns displayed mouths full of long, splintered teeth. They did not look friendly.

"What you dooin' in woods, witch?" one of them snarled.

"Um, we're lost. If you could show us the nearest portal we'll be on our way in a jif—"

Scratching and hissing voices scraped the air as the creatures closed their ring tighter.

"—fy."

Lyra snarled, teeth bared.

The creatures stopped short. "We take witch's magicsss!"

Shaking with fear, Kara pointed her unicorn jewel at the beasts. "You stay away from us!"

The gem crackled with energy as light shot straight up, twisting into a diamond beam. Kara winced as her magic dissolved into fragments, shooting in all directions at once. She'd managed to slow the advance of the tree monsters, but she had not stopped them. Kara would eventually tire, or worse, have to find the ladies room.

Lyra carefully eyed the creatures on the left side. *"When I say so, run."*

"No! I'm not leaving you," Kara declared.

"Comes closer, crispie critter. Looks tasty." Sharp fingers beckoned as the creatures taunted the cat.

Kara looked around desperately. She had to hold her magic together. Lyra wasn't going to win this fight on her own, and without Kara's magic, they were helpless.

"AieOOO!"

A bloodcurdling scream tore through the forest.

Something black flew across the glade, extending a deadly looking sword and swiping it over the creatures' heads. It yelled again, savage and loud.

The tree creatures grumbled angrily but melted back into the shadows of the woods . . . leaving Kara and Lyra alone with this new menace.

The figure let go of a thick vine, landing with a thud on its rump.

Kara's jaw dropped. It was a boy. Well, it looked like a boy. He was covered in black. What she thought had been wings was really a sleek, black cape.

The boy sprang to his feet and bowed deeply. "Good day, milady."

"Who are you?" Kara demanded.

"I am the Forest Prince." The boy stood. "And I am at your service."

"Great, then you can kindly lead me to the nearest portal," Kara responded. She could play this game.

"When you failed to show at the ring, I thought you could be in trouble," he said cheerily. "And by the looks of those wrags, I would say my arrival was quite timely."

Sheathing his sword, the stranger approached Kara. He was dressed completely in black, from boots, pants, and shirt to gloves. A black bandanna around his head concealed even the color of his hair. He looked young, maybe a few years older than Kara, but with a black mask covering his features, it was hard to tell. All Kara could see was a pair of pale green eyes.

Lyra moved in front of Kara, daring the boy to so much as breathe.

"Whoa, nice kitty." The boy raised his arms and took a step back. "The woods are full of magic trackers. Allow me to escort you."

"Okaaay." Whoever this guy was, Kara needed to steer him toward a reality check. "Thanks," she said brightly. "Leave me your e-mail and I'll get back to ya."

He sprang toward her, generating a warning growl from Lyra. "Everyone's waiting for you."

"Exactly! Molly, and Heather, and Tiffany. I've got a play to rehearse for—"

"We must hurry." The boy's voice took on a new tone of urgency as he reached to grab her arm.

"Wait a minute. I'm not going anywhere with you!" Kara declared, hands on her hips. "What's going on here? Where am I? And why are you all dressed like Zorro?"

The boy looked puzzled. "You are in the Fairy Queen's enchanted woods."

When Kara didn't budge, the stranger pressed on. "The Five Kingdoms have gathered to meet you. Any time lost will only goad them toward the path of war."

"I hate to disappoint you, but I'm not staying," Kara answered. "Where's the portal that brought me here?"

The mysterious stranger started canvassing the nearby bright purple bushes, waving his sword this way and that. "No portals connect to the Fairy Realms, Princess."

"Then how did I get here?"

With a *clink,* the sword hit something.

"You arrived here through this."

Kara walked closer and saw the outline of a rectangle set into the ground. It was large, thin, completely flat, with no frame. The gray surface seemed to absorb everything around it, making it virtually invisible. Kara ran her hand over the front, sending ripples fanning out along the surface. Deep silver gleamed beneath, revealing Kara's image like a reflective pool.

"A mirror?" Kara asked.

"We only use mirrors here" the boy explained.

"Then how did those two knuckleheads get in my closet?"

"Ah. The two adventurers Master Tangoo hired to bring you here," Zorro guessed.

"I was kidnapped!" Kara protested.

"The mirror was connected to the portal. Very dangerous way to travel to the Fairy Realms. But you're here." The boy smiled, warm and unthreatening.

"Listen, Forest Gump," Kara said. "How do I go back?"

"Are you a mirror master?"

"No!"

"Then you can't. Only a mirror master can open a traveling mirror to the web."

"Well, stand back, Zorro. I have my own traveling accessories," Kara said. She closed her eyes, fighting the fear creeping along her spine. "Dragonflies! Attention all minis. Front and center!"

Instantly, the air began to bubble. Bright lights erupted like popcorn.

POP! pop! POP! pop! POP!

Five mini dragons dove around Kara, squealing and whirling with excitement. Kara couldn't control all her magic, but at least she could count on the dragonflies. Red Fiona, purple Barney, orange Blaze, and blue Fred all buzzed happily. Yellow Goldie landed and nuzzled Kara's neck. "Kaaraa!"

"I'm glad to see you, too," she cooed, stroking the mini's head. Goldie's golden jewel eyes swirled in pleasure.

The stranger in black gaped at her. "Fairy dragons! Surely you are a princess of magic."

"Yeah, just call me Snow White," Kara quipped. She turned to the dragonflies. "I need you guys to make a portal home, pronto."

The d'flies had helped the mages before by

creating portals for them to jump through—surely they could make one now.

The minis put their heads together, squeaking uncertainly. After a few seconds they locked wing-tips, spinning into a circle. The air between their wings stretched and warped, spitting flashes of jagged light.

"What's wrong, bad reception?" Kara asked.

The dragonflies stopped spinning and faced Kara.

"Nokee dokeee," Barney said sadly.

"Flooieeeee," Blaze added. The other four d'flies nodded in agreement.

"It's too risky for you to use their portal to travel across the web," Lyra interpreted.

Kara couldn't believe it. "How am I supposed to get home?"

"If I may make a suggestion, Princess Snow White," the stranger in black offered, "Tangoo is a very powerful mirror master. He would be able to get you back home."

"How do I find this Tang-dude?" Kara eyed the maze of giant trees stretching in all directions.

"He's at the Fairy Palace. I'll take you."

Kara narrowed her eyes suspiciously. "Why should I trust you if you won't even show your face?"

"Those tree creatures will be back," the boy in black said. "And there are others. Ever since the web went wild, creatures of all sorts have shown up hunting for magic."

Kara sighed. "Okay, but I need to do something first. Don't look!" she warned.

The boy spun around, his back to Kara. "Your wish is my command."

Kara quickly huddled the five minis close together and whispered. "Can you make a d'fly portal phone? *Please* tell me you can at least find Emily and Adriane." The brightly colored dragonflies scrunched their jeweled eyes, working through the challenge, then nodded eagerly. Locking wingtips again, they whirled in a circle.

"No peeking!" she called to the boy, shielding the small window.

Blaze and Fred peeped, signaling a connection had been made. A pulsing light formed in the center of the d'flies' wing circle. Kara held her jewel tight and leaned in close, trying to see what the minis had found.

She looked at a pocked, white surface, indented with rings and rivulets. It moved back and forth, swaying to a beat.

"What is that?" Kara asked, shifting back.

"Deedee!" Fred squeaked.

The craggy image moved, revealing a seat—right in the middle of the school auditorium. Adriane sat forward, her long dark hair spilling over the seat. She slid a pair of headphones to her neck and looked into the portal. Kara had been looking at the bottom of Adriane's sneaker.

"Fred?" Adriane whispered. "Is that you?"

"Is meemee, Deedee," Fred chirped quietly. "KeeKee heer."

"All right, all right, enough with the small talk." Kara pushed her face to the little window. "Hey."

"Kara?" Adriane gasped. "Where are you?

"I'm in the Fairy Realms."

"What!?" Adriane cried, then quickly contained her voice to a whisper. "How did you find a portal?"

"It found me. One opened in my closet, and I fell into it," Kara explained hurriedly.

"Are you okay?"

"Yeah, yeah, fine. Lyra's here with me. No time to explain right now."

"Everyone's expecting you here in like a half hour!" Adriane exclaimed. "Can you get back?"

"Not yet. This is the best the d'flies can do. And Heather, Molly, and Tiffany will be at my house any minute. You have to get over there and cover for me until I can find a way home," Kara said. "Oh, and there's a mookrat and a hobgoblin in my closet. Keep them away from my shoes!"

"Huh?"

The window shifted left as the mini dragons tried to hold it together.

"Wait a minute, who's that?" Adriane could see the boy in black standing patiently to the side.

Kara didn't quite know how to answer. "He's a little light on the shining armor, but he's taking me to some dude to see about getting out of here."

Adriane thought for a second. "Can the d'flies open phone portals to one another if they separate?"

Fiona nodded her little head. "Eezee, keekee."

"Okay, I get your drift." Kara eyed the dragonflies. "We can all keep in contact through d'fly cell phones. Fiona, you go and stay with Emily. Fred, go with Adriane. And Blaze and Barney, go to my room and keep an eye on those two chuckleheads. Goldie stays with me."

"Sounds good," Adriane approved. "And be careful."

Kara nodded. "Okay, d'flies, let's move out."

The window winked out in a flurry of rainbow bubbles, taking four of the five dragonflies with it. Goldie remained, sitting on Kara's shoulder, preening her golden wings.

"Can I turn around now?" the boy in black asked.

"Okay," Kara anwered. "Let's go."

"Right this way, Princess Snow White." Adjusting the silver sword at his side, he started into the woods, Kara and Lyra following close behind. "May I call you Snow?"

"No."

The boy eyed her warily.

"But you *can* call me Kara."

There was no trail, but the stranger strode confidently along a twisting course. The fairy creatures of the forests soon began converging again, following at a distance, scuffling and giggling.

"I've never seen anyone attract so many creatures," the Forest Prince said, walking alongside Kara.

"Back off, bub!" Goldie squeaked harshly.

The boy stepped back. "You have some very loyal protectors."

"And don't you forget it!" Lyra snarled.

Kara gave Goldie a scritch between the mini's wings, the d'fly's favorite scritching spot.

"So, I take it you're from around here?" Kara ventured, hoping to find out something about her mysterious new friend.

He nodded. "I'm familiar with all of the Five Kingdoms in the Fairy Realms."

"Huh?"

"The five major races that live here: Goblin, Troll, Dwarf, Elf, and Fairy," the boy replied, pulling aside a thorny branch hanging in the path. "You should have arrived in the Fairy Ring." He gestured for Kara to walk ahead.

"The what?"

The Forest Prince pointed a black-gloved hand. "There."

Kara squinted through the tree trunks. Stepping

around the giant trees, she stood at the edge of the forest. "Oh . . . my . . . ," she gasped.

Before them stretched an organic city, made entirely of flora. At one end, an enormous palace seemed to grow from the gardens themselves. Deep golden trees formed elegant shining towers, and thick, blooming vines intertwined to make lush green walls. Countless bright flowers adorned the palace, framing arched windows and encircling the high towers. Other structures lay sprawled among the grounds.

"Follow this path through the main gardens," the Forest Prince instructed. "You'll find the Fairy Ring on the far side. Good luck." The stranger in black bowed and began backing into the woods.

"Aren't you coming with me?" Kara asked.

"I can't." He edged farther back into the woods, his masked face hidden in the shadows. "Be seeing you, Princess."

He melted into the darkness and vanished.

"Not if I see you first!" Kara called.

"He did help us." Lyra moved onto a pathway lined by silvery green weeping willows.

"Uh-huh," Goldie concurred.

"Well, if *he'd* been lost in an enchanted mall, I totally would've helped *him.*"

Smoothing her hair, Kara walked forward, Lyra following. She wished she had a comb. A little lip gloss wouldn't hurt, either.

Kara followed a winding path through the gardens. She turned a corner and before her stood a huge, round amphitheater made of purple wisteria vines. Four archways wrapped in bright red and yellow flowers served as entrances and exits to the open-air structure.

Angry voices echoed inside. Kara toyed with her unicorn jewel nervously. The Forest Prince had said she was expected, so she assumed she could get help. But Kara had learned it was dangerous to assume anything when magic was involved.

"I guess we'll just have to announce ourselves," Kara said, walking into the Fairy Ring.

Suddenly Kara stopped in her tracks. A huge gathering of creatures was crowded within. Enormous trolls, green goblins, delicate fairies, squat dwarves, and nimble elves were crammed into the Fairy Ring. Several were standing in the center of the ring, shouting at the top of their lungs.

"I grow weary of waiting!" an angry troll yelled, pacing on huge, knobby feet and waving a giant calloused fist in the air.

"You talk about saving the Fairy Realms, yet each day it grows worse," accused a stout dwarf.

"We demand to know where she is!" an enraged goblin jumped and shouted.

"And so I shall tell you!" a clear voice rang out. The argument instantly ceased. Kara could barely see a tall figure in long robes adorned with strange symbols. Long green hair tied back, his gaunt face sported a goatee, hawkish nose, and deep black eyes that bored straight into Kara. "The answer we have been waiting for is here."

Chapter 3

Kara stood at the arched entrance to the Fairy Ring, shocked and speechless. The only thing anchoring her to reality was Lyra's reassuring presence by her side and Goldie's nervous twittering at her shoulder.

Inside the Fairy Ring, five pairs of thrones grew from the gleaming wood of the structure. The rulers from each of the Five Kingdoms, Elf, Goblin, Fairy, Troll, and Dwarf, occupied the royal pedestals. Circling them, crowds of creatures sat upon tiered toadstool seats, crammed all the way to the top.

A regal woman adorned with a glittering jeweled crown and richly embroidered robes glided gracefully toward Kara. She was a tall, delicate fairy, with flowing hair the color of honey. Sparkling wings of swirling rainbow patterns fluttered at her back. Her rich violet gown accented her almost purple eyes.

She must be a queen, Kara realized.

"Welcome, Princess Kara," the Fairy Queen said, smiling brilliantly.

"Look, she's got a fairy dragon!" A wood nymph stood in the bleachers, pointing a long, green finger.

Goldie waved excitedly. One glittering wing of Kara's costume, already loosened in the forest, ripped off and clattered to the floor.

The mini looked back over Kara's shoulder. "Oops."

The crowd stared at Kara in mute horror. Eyes of all shapes, sizes, and colors widened in disbelief.

"Uh-oh." Kara suddenly got it. These creatures had thought her wings were real!

The Troll King rose from his seat, drawing his bushy eyebrows together in a ferocious scowl. His massive body looked like it was carved from a mountain, with thick gray skin, dark brown hair, and moss green eyes. He wore thick leather armor.

In a voice that sounded like grinding rocks, he laughed. His outburst set off a round of guffaws from the entire troll contingent, all massive brutes.

"Do you mock us?" the Troll King bellowed. "You think this human girl is going to save the Fairy Realms?"

"I would not joke in such dire times, King Ragnar," the Fairy Queen answered respectfully, keeping her eyes on Kara. "This is no ordinary girl."

"She most certainly is not." The tall, wizened, green-skinned goblin walked in front of the queen. Looking down his hawk-like nose, he scrutinized

Kara with sharp, black eyes. He smiled and called to the audience, "This is the blazing star."

Gasps of disbelief ran through the crowd.

"You are quite right, Tangoo," the queen said proudly.

Everyone looked at Kara expectantly. She had no idea what to do.

"I am Queen Selinda," the fairy said softly. "Step forward."

Kara did as she was asked. Gulping, she managed to squeak, "Hi, what's up?"

"Selinda, this is an outrage!" the Goblin Queen shouted. She stood from her throne and walked into the Ring, green cheeks flushed purple with anger, eyes gleaming. A meek-looking Goblin Prince followed behind her. Slicking back black spiky hair with green highlights, the prince placed his other bejeweled hand on the Goblin Queen's shoulder, trying to calm her down.

"Mother, this is the girl chosen by the Fairimentals."

The stout Goblin Queen pushed between her sorcerer and the Fairy Queen to look Kara over. "Where is her mentor?"

Lyra stepped forward with a snarl, making the four back off.

"I would refrain from any more outbursts if I were you, Raelda," Selinda advised, smiling at the big cat.

Flustered, Raelda stepped back.

"My luminous ladies." Tangoo bowed to both queens. "I will guide the girl through the whole thing."

"What's going on here?" Kara asked. "What thing?"

Queen Selinda turned her violet eyes back to Kara and smiled. "I am sorry you were brought here so abruptly. You were supposed to arrive through the mirror here in the Fairy Ring." Selinda pointed to a large mirror set by her throne. Unlike the camouflaged gray glass mirror in the forest, this one was bright silver, elegantly framed by intricate golden flowers.

"Well, I fell out in the middle of the forest," Kara said, irritated.

"Connecting mirrors to portals is not a precise magic," Tangoo explained.

"I would've been blazing stardust if the Forest Prince hadn't rescued me," Kara huffed.

The Fairy Ring suddenly erupted in chaos, everyone shouting and yelling at once.

"She's working with that bandit!"

"What deceit is this?"

"Arrest her at once!"

Kara winced. Goldie squeaked. Lyra stood steady.

"I was attacked by tree wrags," Kara said meekly.

"Wrags in the queen's woods," an elf yelled. "I told you the situation is dire!"

"She is in league with that thief of magic," the Dwarf King spat, leaping up on short, squat legs. He was only as tall as a pixie, but four times more massive, with a long, braided beard on his aged face.

"This boy saved my life," Kara explained. The mystery guy *had* saved her, but Kara had known there wasn't something quite right about him. No one who was being completely truthful needed to hide behind a mask.

"Temperance, Rolok," the Elf King interjected, speaking evenly but firmly to the Dwarf King. The short, kindly elf smiled warmly at Kara, but spoke to the crowds. "The blazing star is a friend to the elves, as are the other two mages, the healer and the warrior."

They knew about Emily and Adriane? Kara thought wildly. What else did they know? And what did they want?

"Let us give the young mage a chance."

"Fine, but she must find the power crystal now," the Goblin King growled. "Or we proceed with our plans to seal off the Fairy Realms from the rest of the worlds!"

"You cannot do that, King Voraxx!" the Fairy Queen entreated. The crescent-shaped jewel on her crown glittered as she looked at the other rulers. "If you seal off the Fairy Realms, the magic web will surely be destroyed and all worlds with it!"

Kara gulped. "*All* worlds, as in Aldenmor, and *Earth?*"

"Sacrifices must be made. We can reconstruct the web," Voraxx insisted stubbornly.

"You don't know if that will work," the Elf King argued.

"We must save ourselves while there is still time!" the Troll Queen shouted in agreement with the Goblin King.

"It is our sworn duty to use Avalon's magic to enrich *all* worlds," the Fairy King interjected.

"The magic runs wild," the Troll King growled.

"Precisely why we need the power crystal to stabilize the Five Kingdoms," Queen Selinda said, keeping her voice calm. "The Fairy Realms depend on magic more than any other place."

"I have authorized Tangoo's plan to bring the blazing star here," Raelda spoke, looking sharply at Selinda. "Let us see if the sorcerer is as smart as he looks."

Selinda's lips twitched in a smile.

"However," Raelda continued. "If she fails, we will do what we must to save ourselves and our lands."

Fairy King Oriel stood and moved to the center of the ring, his sky blue robes rippling around his lithe form. "Anyone who tries to seal off the Fairy Realms will have to deal with me first."

"And the elves," said the Elf Queen firmly, her

distrust of goblins reflected in her brown eyes. "The blazing star proved her courage by sending the magic of Avalon to save Aldenmor. We stand with the fairies!."

The Goblin Queen countered, "If this so-called blazing star had not released the magic of Avalon, we wouldn't *be* in this mess!"

"I didn't know what would happen!" Kara protested.

The Fairy King glowered at Queen Raelda. He spoke in a threatening whisper. "The Dark Sorceress was aided directly by *your* people. I wonder how high up the chain of command that went?"

Realda gasped in shock.

"That is enough!" Selinda commanded. "The mages have already found one of the power crystals."

All eyes focused back on Kara.

She stammered, "My friends and I gave it to the Fairimentals for safekeeping. We're supposed to find the other eight."

The crowd muttered. Some even began laughing again.

The Fairy Queen raised her voice. "Magic attracts magic, and who is more magical than a blazing star?" She looked at the other rulers. "Surely you will give her a chance before we resort to war."

"Why can't you find the power crystal yourself?" Kara asked quietly.

"We've tried," the queen explained. "But without the magic of Avalon, we grow weaker every day. You are the blazing star."

"Show us some magic, blazing star," a nymph called out.

"Er . . . magic?" Kara asked nervously. "I've got dress rehearsal at school in, like, fifteen minutes."

"Let the blazing star prove herself!" the Troll King rumbled.

"Agreed!" the Dwarf King added.

The doubting Goblin Queen stood back and crossed her arms.

Arguing with these fairy creatures wasn't getting Kara home any sooner. Besides, if what they said was true, there might not be a home . . . an earth . . . to go home to. "Lyra, what should I do?" she whispered.

"Stand close to me and we will focus your magic."

Goldie hugged Kara's neck. "I help."

"All right." If she could pull off a tiny bit of flashy blazing star power to dazzle her hosts, maybe they'd help her. She held up the unicorn jewel dangling from her silver necklace. It sparked with power.

Awed by the gem, the crowd fell silent.

"Picture in your mind what you want to accomplish," Lyra advised.

Closing her eyes in concentration, she imagined a beautiful rainbow arcing from her jewel. She reached for Lyra. "Okay, here goes."

ZzzaPPP!

A beam of light shot from the jewel straight above the ring. Fireworks of rainbow sparkles exploded in the air, making everyone duck.

Kara struggled to control her jewel.

Lyra and Goldie tried to help with their own magic, but theirs was like a sprinkle of raindrops on a forest fire.

They want magic, I'll show them magic! Everything seemed to fall away as the white-hot center of Kara's magic flared to life. Power rushed through the very fabric of her being. Diamond fire spun around her body, engulfing her in dazzling spirals. She was a tower of blazing light.

Somewhere through a curtain of bright fire, she saw people running away, horrified by the outburst of such immense power.

Suddenly panic tore through her. Everything she feared about her magic bubbled to the surface and erupted over. She could not hold it—could not control the power.

Screaming, Kara staggered backward, stumbling against Lyra. A jagged bolt blasted from her jewel, sending the crowd scattering.

Pixies dove to the ground. Dwarves rolled head over boots onto outraged fairies, while trolls caught startled hobgoblins flying through the air.

Kara's magic slammed into the bleachers, slicing

through three layers of seats. Uprooted toadstools sent smoldering spotted caps bowling over a group of boggles.

Trying to keep away from the crowd, she spun. The magic smacked into the large mirror, splitting into rainbow shards, and ricocheting everywhere.

A scream of anguish came from behind her. She whipped around to see Lyra bombarded by rainbow fire, turning green, red, orange, purple, and finally blazing silver.

"Kara!"

"Lyra!" Kara shrieked, her stomach burning with panic. Desperately wrenching her magic back, she slammed the fire downward, razing deep slashes across the center of the ring.

"Stop!" Kara screamed. The unicorn jewel suddenly dimmed.

Kara wobbled unsteadily. Lyra! What had she done? Instead of warm orange and black fur, the cat had been transformed into shining silver. Mouth half-opened in a roar, tail held high, Lyra was a frozen, lifeless statue.

"Extraordinary," the Dwarf Queen declared, looking closely at the frozen cat.

"Wow, look at that!"

"She's good to go!"

The crowd broke into excited cries.

Kara burst into tears.

"The girl has obvious power," the Fairy King bellowed, examining the smoking trenches that now scared the ring. "Raw, but impressive."

"Calm, child," Queen Selinda said. "Now turn your friend back."

"I . . . I don't know what I did!" Kara wailed, a distressed Goldie crying on her shoulder.

"Quicksilver," Raelda concluded, examining the frozen cat.

Kara watched in horror as a drop of glimmering silver melted from Lyra's tail and landed in a small puddle on the ground. "What's happening to her?"

"She is melting," Raelda explained unsympathetically.

Kara looked at the crowd through blurred tears. "How do I turn her back?"

The Goblin Prince knelt, studying the Lyra statue. "Tangoo, what say you?"

Kara looked at the young boy: tall, lanky, and—green.

"Hmmm." Tangoo looked over the frozen cat. "I haven't seen this kind of spell in years, Prince Lorren."

"How long do we have?" Selinda asked.

"A day, maybe more," the sorcerer replied casually. "Once the cat melts completely there is no way to counter the spell. But," he added emphatically, "a very powerful gem like the power crystal would cure her for sure."

Kara gulped. This couldn't be happening. But one look at Lyra, melting into the scorched earth, and she knew it really was.

"I suggest we proceed immediately, my lady," Tangoo stepped forward, adjusting his long robes.

Kara's stomach lurched. If he expected her to use magic again, she had no idea what would happen. But she *had* to find the power crystal now!

"The elemental fairy horse is ready and waiting," Tangoo said excitedly. "All she has to do is ride it."

"With such a powerful steed, she will become an even stronger magic magnet," the Elf Queen mused. "The power crystal will surely be drawn to her."

"I can do that," Kara said immediately, so relieved, she almost laughed. This was her big magic thing? Lyra would be cured in no time.

"An excellent idea," the Fairy King approved. "We are all anxious to finally see the horse you have created."

Tangoo smiled smugly. "You will not be disappointed."

"I rode a unicorn across the magic web," Kara boasted, holding out her jewel but quickly pulling it back as the crowd gasped. Giving the kings and queens her best winning smile, she faced the Ring. "I'm an excellent rider. Of course I can ride some cute little fairy pony."

The Fairy Queen addressed the other monarchs.

"We will give Princess Kara twenty-four hours to find the power crystal."

"Agreed. But if the girl fails," the Goblin Queen said, her glimmering green eyes glaring harshly, "we will meet on the battlefield."

The trolls and dwarves rumbled in agreement, but the elegantly dressed Goblin Prince looked queasy, his green eyes wide with fear.

"It will not come to that," the Fairy Queen said confidently. "The blazing star will not fail."

"She has one day!" the Dwarf King said. "Our armies will be ready."

Kara's head was pounding. If she hadn't turned Lyra into a melting statue, she could've walked away from all this and figured out how to get home by herself. She could regroup with Emily and Adriane and they'd work out a plan, like usual. But now she had no choice. She had to save Lyra.

Chapter 4

"It's about time!" Ozzie, the golden brown ferret, had been nervously pacing Kara's front lawn, waiting for Emily and Adriane to show up.

"What's the scoop?" Adriane asked as they quickly made their way up the walkway to the Davies's large tudor home.

"Kara's parents left," Ozzie reported, adjusting the leather collar that secured his golden ferret stone. "Her brother is still inside. Rasha, Ronif, and Balzathar report no activity from the Ravenswood portal."

"So this portal is isolated to Kara's closet," Emily mused.

"She does have a knack for attracting magic," Ozzie continued.

"Any sign of other strange visitors?" Adriane asked, hoping they wouldn't be surprised by other portal-openings.

"Not so far. Dreamer's been canvassing the

grounds." Ozzie waved a paw at the large black wolf pup emerging from the trees.

Dreamer, a mistwolf and natural magic tracker, trotted to Adriane's side, his rich ebony coat shining in the sun. On his chest, a star of snowy white matched the white bands on his paws.

Adriane ran her hand over her pack mate's smooth fur. "What'd you sniff out?"

Scrunching his long nose, the mistwolf's voice echoed in the others' minds. *"Something smells terrible!"*

"Gah!" Ozzie sniffed under his arm. "My shipment of ferret shampoo is behind schedule!"

Emily gave the ferret a stern look.

Adriane hid a smile and nodded at the others. "Let's go." She rang the large brass doorbell.

Almost instantly, the double doors swung open. "Hark, what wind through yonder doorway breaks?" Kyle, Kara's older brother, was doing equal opportunity damage to a chocolate Pop-Tart and Shakespeare. He grinned at them. "Forsooth, it's the odd squad."

"Charming as always, Kyle," Adriane quipped.

"Hey, boy, how you dooin'?" Kyle ruffled Dreamer's head. "What are you feeding him—he's huge!"

"Pooot toots!!" Fred and Fiona squeaked inside Emily's backpack as she struggled to hold it in place.

"Say, you finished with that?" Ozzie asked, eyeing the half-eaten Pop-Tart in Kyle's hand.

"What?" Kyle was confused: Who just said that?

"I said is Kara finished . . . getting ready?" Emily covered up, pushing Ozzie behind her and pointing to his magical ferret stone. He was supposed to use his jewel to speak telepathically when around others.

"The princess is upstairs," Kyle said, wiping sugar sprinkles and wolf saliva from his shirt. "Hey, guess who's here?"

"Who?" Emily asked, anxiously peering beyond Kyle.

"Joey. You've *got* to see his costume!" Kyle walked back toward the kitchen.

"Joey?" Adriane said incredulously. "I just left him backstage. He was setting up the lights—"

"Oh, so that's why you were hanging out in the auditorium," Emily teased, walking into the foyer.

Adriane's cheeks flushed bright red as she followed. "Not! Joey asked me to help him, that's all."

"It's in there." Dreamer pointed his nose toward the kitchen.

Adriane raised her wrist to check her amber wolfstone. The gem was not pulsing. "I don't sense anything dangerous."

"Just be careful." Emily checked her own rainbow jewel. Although hers reacted to animals in distress, it, too, would warn her of impending danger. "These are the first creatures to cross over in months," she continued anxiously. "No telling what kind of magic they have."

The mages entered the kitchen and stifled gasps of shock. A strange-looking boy—really strange—was at the breakfast table, greedily pouring a bowl of cereal into his mouth. Dressed in a weird pirate costume, which included aviator goggles and tan knee-high boots, no one would guess he was human. Which, of course . . . he wasn't.

Two dragonfly heads popped out of Emily's backpack. "Oooo, Froot Loops!"

The costumed creature turned big gray eyes to the group and, "SplOOOF!" spit out the cereal in shock. The bowl crashed to the floor as he leaped to his feet, reaching into his wide utility belt for several colored vials.

"Goblin!" Ozzie yelled, then quickly slapped his paws over his mouth and telepathically added, *"It's a goblin!"*

Adriane instantly swung into a fighting stance, crossing her arms in front of her face. Dreamer crouched to strike, teeth bared, a deep growl rumbling in his throat.

"Mistwolf!" the creature screamed, edging backward and knocking into Kyle.

"Freeze, goblin!" Adriane hissed, her jewel pulsing with restrained fire.

"I'm not a goblin!" The creature raised his hands, eyeing the glowing jewel with fear. "I'm a *hobgoblin!*"

Kyle howled with laughter. "Shakespeare is way cool!" he said, slapping the startled hobgoblin's shoulder.

Emily gently pushed Adriane's arms down. "So, Joey," she said carefully, sending calming magic to Dreamer. "Nice of you to . . . drop in."

"I came for the princess! She is—"

"Yes," Emily cut him off. "We all want to find the princess."

The hobgoblin's eyes narrowed suspiciously. "The reward is already claimed."

"Dude, you're way too into this play," Kyle chortled.

"My name is not Dude," the hobgoblin said, still eyeing the mages warily. "My name is Musso."

HONK! Honk! HONK!

A series of brisk beeps sounded from the driveway, followed by the ringing doorbell.

"There's Kara's ride," Kyle said, jumping to answer the door. "What's taking her so long?"

The minute Kyle walked away, Adriane demanded, "Listen you, whoever you are! Where is our friend?"

"The princess is in the Queen's Fairy Ring," the hobgoblin blurted.

"No she's not, she's in some forest!" Adriane countered.

"Uh-oh." Musso scratched a pointy ear. "The porta-portal must have misfired."

"Who else is with you?" Emily asked.

"Sparky—he's a magic tracker. We are great adventurers. Perhaps you've heard of us?" Musso puffed out his chest. "We rode the web to get the princess."

"You mean kidnap her!" Adriane snapped.

"Yeah!" Ozzie added.

"PhhooooL!" the dragonflies chimed in from inside the backpack.

"How do we get her back?" Emily asked the hobgoblin.

"The portal is moving," he squawked. "I can't tell when it will open again."

"Hark, what reeky, clay-brained, dewberry arrives?" Kyle called from the foyer.

"Stay here!" Adriane warned the hobgoblin.

" 'Course, my calculations could be off—the web is totally flooie," Musso explained. "I have to find the nearest portal!"

The mages raced through the foyer just as Kyle opened the door, bowing deeply. Sparkling fairy wings, silky outfits, and expertly applied glittery makeup twinkled in the morning sunlight.

"I do believe in fairies. I do beliv—"

"Zip it, Kyle," Heather said, stepping past him. "Where's Kara—"

"What are *you* guys doing here?" Tiffany asked. Her pale green brow furrowed as she looked at Emily, Adriane, the golden ferret, and the large black wolf pup.

"Uh, just here to check on Kara," Emily explained.

"Shake a wing, girls," Molly said impatiently, heading for the stairs. "My mom's already late for work."

"Kara's sick," Emily said quickly. "You *really* don't want to go up there."

"She is?" Heather said.

"She is?" Adriane echoed, then caught herself. "Oh, totally."

"She's got a stomach ache," Emily blurted—

Just as Adriane blurted, "Really bad pimple. On her stomach."

"We talked to her, like, fifteen minutes ago, and she was fine." Tiffany swept past Kyle, her pale yellow wing smacking him in the face.

"We'll tell her you were here," Adriane promised, blocking the stairs.

"Jeez, you guys are weirder than normal," Heather said as she and Tiffany and Molly edged past Adriane and trotted upstairs toward Kara's room. "We'll tell her ourselves."

Emily and Adriane ran after them, Dreamer following close.

"Look, it's probably just a little stage fright,"

Tiffany said, her hand already on the door to Kara's room. "She asked us to pick her up."

The mages winced as she flung the door open.

Kara's room was empty.

"K, you in here?" Tiffany asked, scanning the cluttered mess.

"Zzzrrrrp." A sleepy grunt came from a lump under Kara's fluffy pink and white quilt.

Adriane pushed past the trio and dashed inside, pulling the covers down tight as the lump began squirming.

"Hey girl, what's wrong?" Molly asked.

"FooaaaRTT!"

"Bad taco," Adriane yelled as she struggled with the lump.

"Oh Kara, you sound awful!" Tiffany exclaimed.

"You poor thing!" Heather added.

Emily gulped as she saw Barney and Blaze sitting frozen in a pile of Kara's stuffed animals.

"She got sick, like, so totally fast," Tiffany said worriedly.

HONK! HONK! HONK! HONK! HONK!

"Come on, my mom's waiting!" Molly waved a painted green hand.

"Kara, you just rest up," Tiffany said.

"BlaaaaPHH!"

"See, she's feeling better already," Adriane said, smiling.

"We'll check on you later," Heather called out.

"She'll probably be taking a long nap," Emily said, "so just leave her a message."

"Bye!" Emily, Adriane, and the d'flies chorused, cheerful smiles plastered on their faces.

As soon as Heather, Tiffany, and Molly closed the door behind them, Adriane yanked the quilt back. A long, whiskered nose popped out, attached to a big, fuzzy head.

"What are you trying to do, smother me?" the mookrat demanded, whiskers twitching. His beady eyes widened as he saw three magic jewels trained on him.

"Ahhh!" He dove back under the covers.

"Come out of there," Emily said. "We're not going to hurt you."

"Much," Adriane added.

The mookrat stuck his nose out again and took in the group. "Sparky's the name," he said, quivering voice muffled by the quilt. "Magic's my game."

"We just heard the news," said a new voice from Kara's window. A little figure made of twigs and moss was perched atop a beautiful white owl.

"Just in time, Tweek," Emily exclaimed, walking over to the little Earth Fairimental. "Hi, Ariel," she greeted the magical snow owl.

The owl ruffled her feathers, displaying shimmering streaks of gold, lavender, and turquoise. *"That is not Kara,"* the owl observed, liquid eyes looking accusingly at Sparky.

"It's the mookrat who kidnapped Kara!" Ozzie informed her, glowering.

"We were hired to find her," Sparky protested, pointing his nose toward Kara's closet. "We followed the portal into that chamber."

Tweek leaped from the owl and dashed into the closet. Lifting a sparkling turquoise jewel from a chain about his neck, he started scanning Kara's shoes. "Hmmm, magical residue."

"Stay here with Barney and Blaze!" Adriane ordered the EF and Ariel. "If this mookrat moves a whisker, you call us."

"We have to get that hobgoblin," Emily said.

"There's one," Ariel said, perched on the windowsill.

"What?"

The group rushed to the window. In the driveway, Kyle was climbing into Molly's mom's minivan. Musso clambered in behind him, hands poised by his utility belt full of strange vials. He slid the door closed just as the minivan pulled out of the driveway.

"Oh no!" Emily groaned. "Kyle's taking a hobgoblin to school!"

❁ ❁ ❁

Kara followed Queen Selinda, King Oriel, and Tangoo along a path surrounded by bright wildflowers. The path wound through the gardens, leading to the fairy stable.

The Fairy Queen led Kara to a beautiful stall made of glossy green ivy and daisies. Inside, a pale green horse with bright flowers in her lustrous mane stuck her head over the half-door and nuzzled the queen's face lovingly.

"This is Gaia, an Earth Elemental Horse," the Fairy Queen said, laughing as the mare turned curious azure eyes to Kara.

"Welcome, blazing star."

Kara smiled and petted Gaia. The animal's strong magic was warm and pure. She instantly felt a little better. Everyone had acted like this was going to be such a big deal, but she could totally ride this nice horse. Lyra was going to be saved even sooner than she'd hoped.

"Should I just ride her now?" Kara asked.

Selinda shook her head. "Gaia is my horse. Elemental horses only bond with one rider."

"Oh." Kara was a little disappointed, but there were probably pretty horses just like Gaia in the other stalls.

King Oriel reached into a stall of gleaming crystal to pet a powerfully built silvery blue horse. "This is Frost, a Water Elemental Horse. We've been bonded since I was a child."

"The blazing star will make a strong rider." Frost's sapphire eyes regarded her thoughtfully.

Kara smiled, then frowned. Frost was bonded to

the Fairy King. She wasn't going to be riding him, either. Where was *her* elemental horse?

Boom!

A huge blast shook the corridor, followed immediately by loud cries and snorting from somewhere outside the stables.

Queen Selinda walked straight toward the commotion, leaving the stables through the rear doorway.

Kara followed. Out back, a dark and ominous stall stood isolated from the others. Kara couldn't tell exactly what the structure was made of, but it looked like thick gleaming black glass. It was completely enclosed except for a small window set in the front door.

Tall fairies standing guard yelped as a jet of fire erupted from the open window.

Goldie quivered and grabbed a talon full of Kara's hair to hide behind.

Whatever was in there was angry. Best to keep away from that one, she thought.

The door buckled as something slammed into it from inside. An eye, wide with terror, appeared in the small window. Kara felt a jagged bolt of fire rip through her body, as if her blood were boiling. She gasped, feeling her magic swirling inside, climbing to a fever pitch—it felt like it was going to explode!

Then in an instant it vanished. The window was empty.

"What's in there?" Kara asked breathlessly. "A manticore?"

Tangoo grinned proudly. "This, Princess Kara, is *your* horse!"

Chapter 5

The Stonehill Middle School auditorium buzzed with activity. Backstage, it was jammed with costumed students preparing for dress rehearsal. It wasn't going to be easy for Emily and Adriane to find their runaway hobgoblin.

"Our fairies are here," Adriane noted dryly, pointing to center stage.

Molly, Heather, and Tiffany were putting finishing touches on the Fairy Ring set. It was decorated with bright silk flowers and papier-mâché toadstools, with a backdrop of painted forest trees.

"Whatsup?" Joey—the real Joey—approached, carrying a box of lightbulbs. He smiled broadly at Adriane. "Good call on the bulbs—the ones I was using were way too low wattage."

"Cool," the warrior answered, still scanning the auditorium.

"What foul news!" someone cried in a loud, grating voice. "Our Fairy Queen hath fallen ill! We cannot read this scene without Queen Titania!"

Incoming: Rae Windor, student director of the

play. She glared at the mages, irritation blazing in her steely eyes.

"Alack, poor Kara," Emily called out.

Rae grasped her frizzy brown hair and scowled at Joey. "Whither wander you? You're playing Puck and you're onstage in five minutes! Get ready!"

Joey shrugged. "I gotta change. See you guys later." He hurried off stage right—just as Musso emerged from stage left with Kyle.

The hobgoblin's eyes widened as he took in the scenery. "A Fairy Ring!"

"Hark! Shall I compare thee to a brick outhouse?" Kyle quoted from his Make Your Own Shakespeare Insults book.

Rae glowered. "That is so not hilarious."

"Sure it is. Right, Joey?" Kyle asked the hobgoblin.

Rae's eyes widened. "Forsooth! That's the fastest costume change I've ever seen. You'll make a perfect Puck."

A fairy rushed across the stage. "Have you the heard news about the Fairy Queen?"

"Everyone's heard," a girl dressed in a toga chimed in dramatically. "She is deathly ill."

"The queen is sick?" cried the hobgoblin. "This is terrible news! Not with the fairy wars brewing!"

Adriane and Emily needed to run interference. Fast. They hurried over. "*Joey,* could we speak to you for a minute, alone?" Adriane asked.

Kyle stepped back, grinning. "Don't let me get in the way of true love, Romeo. Break a leg."

"Break your own leg!" Musso grumbled angrily.

Rae grabbed Musso. "Joey, stand in for the Fairy Queen in this scene."

Musso flailed as Rae dragged him onstage "But it's illegal to impersonate royalty! I'll be turned into a flobbin!"

Emily and Adriane tried to snatch Musso back, but Rae raised her hand imperiously. "Only actors onstage! Places, everyone." She clapped, herding Molly, Tiffany, and Heather. "Mustardseed, Peaseblossom, Cobweb, into position."

"Where's Nick Bottom?" Rae looked around as she pushed Musso to center stage.

"Ready, milady." Marcus, a friend of Kyle's, was playing the role of Nick Bottom, the character in the play who turns into a donkey after a spell is cast on him. He stopped next to the mages. "I heard Kara has some rare disease!"

"Oh, great," Adriane said, and rolled her eyes.

"What Fairy Ring is this?" Musso gaped as he stepped onto the fake flowerbed. "Where's the magic mirror?"

"Stick to the script!" Rae yelled. She gestured to another boy standing offstage. "King Oberon, front and center! Okay, now this is your big scene, where you cast a love spell on Queen Titania. And when Nick Bottom comes out, he'd better be wearing his donkey costume. Got it? And . . . action!"

Adam, a cute eighth grader dressed in the flowing robes of a fairy king, adjusted his golden crown and stepped onstage.

Musso yelped, diving face first while grabbing the boy's legs. "O great Fairy King," the hobgoblin groveled. "I have traveled the web and found the Fairy Princess."

"Hey man, take it easy, Joey!" Adam hopped up and down, trying to shake Musso loose.

Rae got frantic. "People! Stop adlibbing!" She shoved Musso facedown into the bed of silk flowers. "Stay there and don't move!"

Musso lay in the flowerbeds, eyes darting left and right. "The Fairy Ring has been infiltrated," he mumbled.

Adam cleared his throat and read his lines in a loud, clear voice.

" 'What thou seest when thou dost wake,

Do it for thy true love take . . . ' "

Musso dug frantically in his utility belt. "I must protect the Fairy Ring!"

" 'Pard, or boar with bristled hair,

In thy eye that shall appear. . . . ' " Adam recited.

Musso held out a small, round vial. It glowed briefly.

"What's he doing?" Adriane asked, startled as her wolf stone pulsed, signaling danger.

"He's using some kind of magic!" Emily exclaimed.

"The fairies will reward me generously for dealing with spies!" Musso cried out.

" 'When thou wak'st, it is thy dear.

Wake when some vile thing is near.' "

Musso lobbed the glowing green orb at Adam. "I'll show you a vile thing!"

Racing over from the wings, Adriane and Emily swung their wrists up. Glimmering gold and blue light streamed toward the stage, shielding the unsuspecting Adam from whatever Musso's spell was about to do.

With a *twink,* the green spell ricocheted off the mages' shield and flew offstage.

"Very cool lighting, Joey." Adam gave him props. "Really rad."

"That was close," Emily said, letting out a breath as the shield faded.

PooF!

A flash of green light erupted offstage.

"Uh-oh." Adriane grimaced.

"Okay, Nick Bottom, you're on!" Rae ordered.

"HEE-HAW!"

A loud donkey bray echoed throughout the auditorium, making everyone jump. Marcus stumbled onstage, tugging at the ears on his donkey-head costume.

"Excellent!" Rae said. "Best interpretation of a jackass I've seen since Kyle Davies. And . . . action!"

"HeeHawww!" Marcus tried to read a line, stumbled across the set, tripped over Musso, and flew backstage next to Adriane and Emily.

"Marcus, are you okay?" Adriane asked.

"Never better, why?" He scratched his ears and continued to read his lines. " 'I see their knavery.' "

Adriane tried to pull off his mask. It wouldn't budge.

" 'This is to make an ass of me, to fright me, if they could.' HeeHaWW!" brown fur covered Marcus's shoulders and arms.

"Musso's spell!" Emily's hand flew to her mouth as she watched Marcus's tail swish behind him.

"It turned Marcus into a real donkey!" Adriane cried.

❂ ❂ ❂

Kara watched anxiously as the black glass cage was pushed into the riding arena on huge rollers. Rocky walls several stories high circled the stadium. The arena bleachers were filling fast with the kings and queens of the Fairy Realms, and all their entourages.

"Everyone will be perfectly safe when the shield goes up," Oriel reassured Kara.

Safe from a horse? She bit her lip. "What kind of horse is this?"

"He is a fire stallion," Tangoo replied proudly. "One of a kind, forged from the very heart of elemental fire magic."

"Do not worry, Princess," Queen Selinda murmured. "The stallion cannot get out."

"Neither can I," observed Kara.

"I have faith in you," the queen said as she gracefully headed toward her seat.

As the guards placed the glimmering cage and its angry occupant into the center of the arena, Kara thought about the Firemental that had once paid her a visit in the Ravenswood Library. Composed of free-flowing elemental magic, the creature was dangerous and unstable, but it had helped her. How she wished she were back in the warmth of that room now, safe with her friends.

She looked to the brave little dragonfly on her shoulder. "Goldie, I want you to leave—"

"Stay with Kaaraa!" the dragonfly protested, gripping Kara's shoulder.

"Thank you," Kara said softly, petting the mini's head. She was grateful for all the magical help she could get. In fact . . . "Goldie, can you call Fiona?" Kara asked. She held her jewel tightly. "I need to talk to Emily, and fast!"

"Okieee-dokieee." Goldie positioned close to Kara's ear, softly squeaking a series of beeps. "Kaaraa for emeee," the mini whispered.

Kara heard an answering peep.

"Hello?" Kara said tentatively.

"Kara?" Emily's voice floated near Kara's ear, surprised and relieved.

The blazing star jumped. "Emily, it's me!" Kara whispered into Goldie's yellow belly.

"Are you okay?" Emily asked.

Kara fought back tears. "No! I turned Lyra into a quicksilver statue, and she's melting!"

"Oh no!" The healer's voice echoed with concern.

"I don't have much time. I have to bond with an elemental horse to save Lyra," Kara explained hurriedly. "What should I do?"

"Deep breath, Kara," Emily urged her friend. "Magical animals love you. You've already bonded with Lyra, the dragonflies—not to mention half the unicorn population."

The fire horse snorted and kicked wildly inside his cage. Kara gasped for air. "That's different."

"No, it's not," Emily continued, calm but firm. "Trust is everything. Open yourself. Feel what the horse is feeling."

Kara let out a long breath. "Okay."

"Kara, we'll get you home! Don't panic—"

"Good luck, Princess, you'll need it!" the guards yelled, fleeing the arena.

Sparkling beams crisscrossed the air, forming a

glittering dome that enclosed the arena. It was some kind of force field trapping the horse inside. And Kara with it.

"Emily!" Kara cried urgently, but the connection to her friend was lost.

With a violent flash, the front of the black cage fell away.

"Ahhh!" Goldie dove behind Kara, who staggered as intense heat blasted from the open stall. Something seared through her, piercing her mind, burning away any resistance she could offer. Then a wave of power broke over her, pulling her down as if she were caught in a riptide.

A blur of bright orange surged from the stall and flew across the sand. Choking, her eyes watering, Kara squinted through clouds of dust and smoke.

Beyond the shield, the crowd surged to its feet, awed by the sight of the powerful creature.

He was huge—almost twenty hands high. Blazing plumes of flame swirled from his body. He snorted, and smoke billowed from flared nostrils. Hooves of molten lava pawed the sand; strong legs nervously danced. His crackling mane and tail thrashed fire. Kara struggled for breath. She had seen many magical creatures, but the thing standing before her was beyond her wildest dreams.

The horse was made entirely of fire.

The stallion's wild eyes, smoldering like golden coals, turned—and caught Kara in an iron grip of power. She stumbled forward as diamond fire erupted from her jewel, running up her arms and swirling around her body.

Kara hadn't meant to retaliate, but her magic tore across the sand and slammed into the stallion. Rearing in defiance, fire exploded from his body. Searing heat practically singed Kara's hair as the creature towered above her and Goldie.

"I'm sorry," she cried to the stallion. "I can't stop it!"

A second bolt from Kara exploded like fireworks, sending the stallion staggering back.

With all her might, Kara willed her jewel to stop.

"Nice horsie," she croaked, clinging to Emily's advice. Open yourself. Kara stepped forward.

The horse reared back.

"Stay away from me!" the stallion's voice roared through Kara's mind.

She felt the sheer force of the horse's rage surging through her own body. The stallion raced around the perimeter in a blur of reds and orange.

This is good, she told herself, trying to calm her mounting terror. Any breakthrough is good.

Grasping her unicorn jewel tight, she thought of Lyra. Kara always felt so protected, so safe, when her friend was near. Gathering her courage, she advanced toward the horse.

He snorted and backed away, stirring trails of scorched earth.

"I know you don't trust anyone," Kara said soothingly, willing the stallion to feel the friendship she was offering. She pleaded with all her heart. "But my friend is hurt, and if I don't ride you, she is going to die."

The horse held steady; he did not back away this time.

Encouraged, she took a step closer.

"I am fire!" the horse thundered.

The unicorn jewel flared white-hot in her hands as a whirlwind of feelings bore into her like a drill. Hopelessness, fury, confusion, pain, and overwhelming sadness.

"I run alone!"

Trails of fire streaming from his mane, hooves, and tail, the horse charged straight toward her.

The crowd broke out in pandemonium, yelling in fear for the girl.

Before Kara could think, the stallion was on her. She screamed, and diamond fire erupted from the unicorn jewel, slamming into the horse with the force of a cannon. The horse fell headfirst, sending dust and debris flying as it dug a smoking trench into the ground.

"I'm sorry!" the blazing star cried, tears streaming down her dirt-streaked face as the horse staggered to his feet.

Somewhere through the buzzing in her ears, she heard the crowd panicking.

"That's enough!"

"Get her out of there!"

"She'll be killed!"

Guards were running toward them, long spears with sparkling blue tips held high.

"No!" Kara screamed. "Leave him alone!" She reeled, half-blinded as the magic swelled inside her. She struggled to separate her feelings from the stallion's, but he bore down harder, overwhelming her. Kara's heart threatened to break apart as the horse's despair filled her being. She *was* the stallion, trapped, desperate, and alone.

More than anything, she wanted to be free.

Kara's eyes locked onto the stallion's. The truth hit her.

The stallion couldn't control his immense power—just as she could not control hers.

The unicorn jewel erupted, blasting diamond fire into the shield in an explosion of blinding colors.

"Stop! Please!" she cried out. But the magic kept flowing, stronger and stronger, as if there were no end to the ocean of power within her. Kara swooned, terrified. Without Emily and Adriane at her side, she was losing herself.

The shield exploded in splinters of light, disintegrating as horrified onlookers scrambled from the bleachers.

The fire stallion leaped to freedom, fiery muscles

careening over the fleeing crowd in a single bound. Like a flash of lightning, the horse vanished.

The last thing Kara realized before she blacked out was that she was lying on the ground, Goldie circling overhead frantically calling out her name.

Chapter 6

Kara was floating. Long, golden hair swirled around her head as she bobbed gently upon a sea of night. Stars winked faintly, falling in and out of focus.

"Still trying to play with your magic," a familiar voice chided.

The stars pulsed and formed a shifting kaleidoscope. Though fragmented, Kara could make out three figures. They were all draped in long dark cloaks, cowls covering their heads.

One was large, an unnatural bulk shifting beneath the robes; one was tall and lithe, her long, silver hair streaked with jagged lighting. The third—Kara gasped, repulsed by the image of a large cockroach. Oily wings jittered. Antennae twitched.

"How did you find me?" Kara croaked as she tried to crawl away. A shiver ran down her spine.

"My dear girl." The voice was calming, engulfing, drawing her in. "You so underestimate your power. It is like a beacon. No one else could possibly have that signature."

Kara reached for the shifting rainbow lights, but it was like trying to grasp smoke.

"There's so much more to magic than talking to cute animals, isn't there?"

Kara flashed on Lyra, melting away. Her fault. She didn't deserve magic.

"So many willing to risk everything for a taste of your power," the Dark Sorceress said softly. "Everyone uses the blazing star."

Kara could almost feel the cold breath in her ear.

"Until there is nothing left."

Soon Lyra would be nothing. Kara struggled to move.

"Don't you worry your pretty little head. We're going to help you."

Above her, the light blossomed, forming an exquisite flower. Kara struggled to reach its spreading petals—

"Just as you will help us."

—and opened her eyes, disoriented. Her heart pounded as she struggled to unwind herself from her voluminous costume. Where was she? She was safe at home, dreaming, in her own comfy bed! Relieved, she smiled and rolled onto her back. And looked up startled. Twined tree branches, golden and shimmering like sunlight, lined the ceiling. This wasn't her room at all.

Urgent whispers broke through her jumbled thoughts. Someone was in here with her.

"What if it's a sleep spell?" a chirpy voice asked worriedly.

"Oh no! That could last a hundred years!" another voice, this one high-pitched, exclaimed.

"That's absurd! She's not enchanted," a third voice added.

"I think she's up!"

"Someone go look."

"No way. I'm not messing with that fairy dragon."

Kara lifted her head from a lavender-scented silken pillow and looked around. Her eyes found Goldie patrolling the foot of the big bed, marching back and forth.

"Goldie," Kara rasped.

Startled, the d'fly squeaked and leaped. "Kaaraa!" Goldie dove, clasping her wings around Kara's neck in a tight embrace.

"I'm so happy to see you," Kara said, hugging her little friend tight.

Kara noticed the walls and floor were made of the same interwoven trees as the ceiling. Here and there lush bluebells and foxgloves peeked between the golden bark, brightening the room with rainbow-hued petals. Thick rugs in vibrant colors covered the floor.

"Goldie, what's happened?" Kara asked. "What am I doing here?"

"I told you it wasn't a sleep spell," a voice whispered.

"Who's there?" Kara demanded, instinctively grabbing her unicorn jewel. She swung her feet to the floor and carefully stood up, surveying the room. But no one else was there.

She walked to the open double windows. Outside, the moon was rising, casting a silver sheen over the magnificent fairy gardens. She must have been out for hours. She remembered now. She was stuck in the Fairy Realms, and had failed to bond with the fire stallion. The Fairy Realms would go to war, possibly destroy each other—and the worlds she loved—and Lyra would melt into nothing.

"Look at that jewel!"

Kara went rigid. The voices were louder now, closer.

A large oak vanity table carved from an entire tree grew straight up from the floor. A chair sat before it, facing an oval mirror ringed with purple heather. Kara caught her reflection and grimaced. The girl staring back at her was a mess! She was covered in dust and grime. Her hair was matted in a tangle of knots. Her Fairy Queen costume was ripped and filthy.

"Stop squirting me, Whiffle!"

"Oh, I can't stand it!" another voice whispered loudly. "I'm delirious with excitement."

Kara rubbed her eyes. The voices seemed to be coming from the top of the vanity table. Was she still dreaming?

An odd assortment of accessories lined the top

of the vanity below the mirror: a jade green brush, a silver comb with long handle, a gold clamshell mirror, and a quivering white powder puff.

"For a second there I thought *they* were talking," she muttered to Goldie, shaking her head at the ridiculous idea.

Goldie nodded. "Uh honk!"

Or not.

Suddenly the big white powder puff launched itself from the vanity top and flew at Kara's face in a sparkly white cloud.

"Ahhhh!" Kara ducked. The powder puff collided in midair with Goldie.

"Eeeeee!" the mini screamed, furiously flapping sparkly powder-coated wings as she and the powder puff plummeted downward. Goldie landed on the puffball, releasing a lushly scented cloud. Kara watched in amazement as the powder puff wriggled like an excited puppy.

"Bad Puffdoggie!" a voice scolded.

Now who said that?

Kara gaped in disbelief. The silver comb walked across the dresser on two legs formed by its long handle! Glowering at the shaggy powder puff, the comb cleared its throat and took a deep bow. "A thousand apologies, Princess, and allow me to say I am shocked by this most unseemly behavior."

"Whoa, what are you?" Kara blurted.

"We are designed to serve the Fairy Princess," the silver comb said proudly. "My name is Angelo."

"What if that's not she?" the clamshell mirror wailed, and snapped shut.

"Of course it's she, Mirabelle!" the green brush shouted at the mirror, exasperated.

"Well, yeah, I guess I am, that is . . . ," the blazing star stammered, twirling the diamond-bright unicorn jewel between her fingers. "My name is Kara, and this is Goldie."

"We've been waiting a hundred and twenty-five years to serve a Fairy Princess! I'm so happy I could cry!" Mirrabelle started bawling.

An atomizer spray bottle shaped like a skunk shuffled along the table. "I am Whiffle, and I shall make you smell divine." The glass skunk squirted an amazingly lush perfume from his nose.

The brush pushed the atomizer away, hopping up and down on her handle "Can't you see the princess needs immediate attention!"

"Skirmish, calm down," the silver comb said, sighing. "That's why we're here."

Kara self-consciously ran fingers through her tangled tresses. "It's been, like, hours since I even brushed my hair."

The accessories gasped in horror.

"Tell me about it," she said.

"This is no way to welcome our new princess!" Angelo scolded the others, trying to move them back in an orderly line. "Forgive them for not following protocol, Princess Kara, but Queen Selinda ordered us into service on such short notice."

Puffdoggie hopped up and down excitedly, sending sparkling powder flying.

Oh, this is great, Kara thought. Locked away in a tree house with a bunch of enchanted toiletries! Could things get any stranger?

THWAP! BoNnk!

Without warning, a scraggly, bespectacled flying creature zoomed through the open window, smacked into the far wall, and landed in a crumpled heap on the floor.

"Ow."

"Oh!" Kara rushed over and knelt by the creature. "Are you all right?"

It looked vaguely like an owl, with a combination of dark gray fur and moss green feathers. Long, floppy ears drooped forward, half-covering luminous yellow eyes.

Goldie immediately stepped between it and Kara.

The bird straightened his small glasses. Dazed yellow eyes wobbled and then focused sharply on the dragonfly. "You are the Fairy Princess Kara?" he demanded querulously.

Goldie pointed at Kara.

"Oh." The bird reached into a leather shoulder pouch and withdrew a rolled-up piece of black parchment tied with a dark purple ribbon. "I had to try three windows before I found this one!" the creature huffed, struggling to his feet and handing Kara the scroll.

"Thank you, um . . . ," Kara began. "Who are you?"

"Alwyn, Secret Fairy Air Delivery, Second Division," the creature supplied, then continued his complaints. "Royal deliveries are most difficult. You never know what kind of fairy guards are out there!"

"Would you like something to drink?" Kara gestured to a table on the opposite side of the room, piled high with brightly colored fruits and a large bowl of sparkling purple liquid.

"Don't mind of I do," Alwyn grumbled, heaving himself into the air. He landed with a giant splash in the middle of the punch bowl and sighed happily. "Ooo, that feels good."

The enchanted accessories gathered around as Kara slipped the ribbon off the parchment and carefully unrolled it. Glowing purple and silver calligraphy shimmered from the black paper:

MIDNIGHT MASQUERADE RAVE

TONIGHT @ THE FAIRY ISLE—BY INVITATION ONLY

"A party!" Skirmish shrieked, falling off the table in her excitement.

"That's no ordinary party, it's a fairy rave!" Whiffle cried eagerly.

"Yaaaay!!" The accessories all jumped up and down.

"Who sent this?" Kara asked the strange bird.

"Turn it over," Alwyn answered, floating on his back and gargling

Kara flipped the invitation over. On the back was a handwritten note: *If you want to help Lyra, meet me at the rave. The Forest Prince.*

The Forest Prince. He'd saved her life, but everyone at the Fairy Ring had called him a thief. Could she trust him? And a secret midnight rave didn't sound exactly aboveboard. Still, if he could tell her how to help Lyra . . .

Alwyn hauled himself out of the bowl and leaped to the windowsill. "Back to work—I still have many more invitations to deliver. Your ride will pick you up at eleven-thirty sharp." With that, the bird fell out the window and dropped like a stone. "Ahhh, wet wing, wet wing!"

"Wait!" Kara cried, running to the window as the gray and green creature careened crookedly across the fairy gardens. She turned, stomped back, and flopped facedown on the bed.

"Are you going?" Mirabelle asked excitedly, her small round mirror flashing.

"Look at me," Kara cried into the pillow. "How can I possibly go to a party?"

Angelo and Skirmish leaped onto the bed and began inspecting the princess up and down.

"Hmmm, yes, this is a challenge," Angelo concluded, and snapped to attention. "Puffdoggie, prepare the princess's bath at once!"

The powder puff bounced into an adjoining room. Kara heard water filling a tub.

"I can't wear this," Kara groaned, "and I don't have anything else." She flopped backward on the bed. Her beautiful dress was ruined.

"If you will please follow me, Princess." Angelo jumped off the bed and walked to a golden door in the left corner of the room.

"A Fairy Princess closet?" Kara could totally go for that. There were bound to be dozens of gorgeous gowns in there.

She flounced over and flung the door open excitedly.

"It's empty!" she wailed, looking inside the vacant, white-walled closet.

"Well, of course it is!" Skirmish said. "Step inside and tell it what you want!"

"No way!" Kara walked inside, Goldie chirping excitedly on her shoulder.

The closet expanded, instantly surrounding them with gleaming walls. The rest of her bedroom disappeared, leaving only she, Goldie, and the enchanted accessories in a bright white void.

Kara cleared her throat and said, "I want a costume."

In a burst of twinkles, a black and white cow costume appeared and rotated slowly in midair.

"Hee heee," Goldie chuckled.

"Not *that* kind of costume!" Kara said.

Mirabelle snapped open and closed. "The princess needs beautiful dresses!"

The cow costume disappeared, and dozens of glittering ballgowns of various designs and colors twirled before her wide eyes. This was more like it.

"No, no, no! Be gone!" Skirmish commanded.

The rows of dresses vanished, and Kara frowned, dismayed.

"She needs something different, something that will make her really stand out in a crowd!" the brush continued.

Another burst of twinkles morphed into an outrageous orange sequined suit with a pair of stilts.

Kara and Goldie looked at each other and shook their heads dismissively.

Angelo clapped his feet. "Something in a more classic style!"

A drab dress of dark blue with a high collar and straight skirt rotated in the air.

"Much better," the comb said happily. "Elegant and understated."

"And boring," Kara commented. It was time she took things into her own hands, now that she saw how this worked. Standing in the center of the closet, she called out, "I need a ballgown in violet silk, with an embroidered bodice, long sleeves, and a dropped A-line skirt."

A richly colored dress materialized and spun in the air. It looked exactly as Kara had envisioned it.

"Marvelous!" Skirmish cried.

"Inspired!" Angelo exclaimed.

Puffdoggy barked in agreement.

"Wait!" Tapping fingers to her lips, Kara considered. "It needs something else." She put her fashion sense into overdrive. "Emerald, sapphire, and yellow topaz beading along the bodice."

"Ooooo." The accessories swooned at the swirling patterns of glittering gems.

The color theme gave Kara another idea. "Peacock feathers along the back of the neck and embroidered on the cuffs, and a violet satin mask with peacock feathers to match."

Kara's alterations magically appeared, until the most amazing dress she'd ever seen twirled gracefully before her eyes.

"She is a genius!" Whiffle cried. "An auteur!"

"I *so* have to get one of these closets at home," Kara exclaimed, overawed.

"Shoes!" Goldie squeaked.

"How could I forget the best part?" Kara gratefully hugged the mini. "With matching purse!"

By the time she was through, she had a pair

of purple satin slippers with two-inch-high square heels, each glittering with a jeweled peacock feather.

"Amazing!" Mirabelle whispered. "Your fashion magic is unequaled in the Fairy Realms."

"And on Earth." Kara bowed.

"Come, we must bustle!" Angelo clapped his feet. "Princess, in there!" Angelo pointed his comb-teeth to the steam-filled bathroom and the large golden tub in its center. "The rest of you"—he pointed to the others—"let's get busy!"

The accessories quivered with excitement as they prepared Kara's magical makeover.

Once totally scrubbed and squeaky clean, Kara sat in a fluffy pink robe at the vanity, munching on sweet fruits and flaky pastries. Skirmish dove into her hair with a wild cry and twirled among her tresses, creating gorgeous looping curls on the right side of her head. Angelo combed the left side straight until it gleamed like a sheet of gold. Comb and brush glared angrily at each other when they saw what the other had done, and started tussling.

Mirabelle flapped open, and iridescent sparkling eyeshadow soared out, dusting Kara's lids. The eye-shadow's opalescent shine highlighted her blue eyes perfectly.

"And now for the dress." Kara disappeared behind a vine-covered dressing screen in the corner of the room and emerged a moment later. She reached up to the curls piled high atop her head.

"No!" Skirmish cried. "I've been fighting tangles all my life, and I know what's what. Don't touch anything!"

Kara smiled, tugging free a lock at her temple. It spiraled down, gently framing her face.

"Except that!" Skirmish was beside herself. "You are a diva, my lady!"

"One final touch." Whiffle spritzed a pink mist. A wonderful scent of jasmine enveloped Kara, with a hint of citrus to balance the sweetness.

"It's incredible, Whiffle!" Kara exclaimed.

"I know," the crystal atomizer sniffed. "I call it 'Morning Pew.' "

Carefully arranging the peacock mask, Kara surveyed the final effect. The rich colors of her dress set off her gleaming blond hair and sparkling blue eyes.

"Hey, where's Goldie?"

The closet door swung open, and Goldie appeared, decked out in a glittering silver and gold lamé tuxedo, complete with a feather mask.

"Perfect!" Kara squealed, clapping her hands.

Unable to control themselves, the accessories burst into a rousing cheer as Kara and Goldie pirouetted in front of the mirror.

"Da bomb!" Skirmish and Angelo cried happily—for once in absolute agreement.

Something darker than the night alighted just outside the window. Large as a horse with shimmering black wings, a giant bat creature turned bright green eyes to Kara.

"Princess, your ride is here," Angelo announced.

Kara nodded. She was ready to go.

Chapter 7

Kara gripped the leather saddle as the large bat creature sliced through thin clouds into silvery night sky. Below were lush forests, and every so often, mysterious glades hidden in star shadow. Dark mountains ringed the distance, hugged by billowing clouds, deep and thick barriers at the edge of the world.

With a slight rumble, the bat ducked its head and swooped low, gliding over a huge lake that gleamed like liquid moonlight. In the distance, a mist-shrouded island rose from the luminous waters. Ablaze with lights, the isle twinkled like a floating jewel.

The bat glided onto smooth silver stones near the lakeshore, setting down neatly between a giant Pegasus and a flying carpet. Music echoed across the still waters.

"Thanks." Kara patted her steed's leathery neck as she slid to the ground and straightened her dress. She looked up in awe. Hordes of costumed creatures were entering through a crystal archway. She had no idea what kinds of creatures hid beneath the elaborate disguises and sparkling masks; it was probably just as well.

Relax, Kara told herself. Parties were her natural environment. If anyone knew how to handle a tricky social situation, it was her.

"Let's get this party started," she told Goldie and walked briskly through the arch—and straight into the wildest party she had ever seen! Music thundered, pounding across the open glade. Floating fairy lanterns strobed deep colors across a mass of costumed fairy creatures rocking out on the dance floor. The place was jammed!

"Goldie, see if you can spot mystery guy," Kara said, searching high and low among the costumed throngs.

The d'fly took off just as dozens of small winged fairies glided over Kara, dusting her with twinkles of lights. Goldie twirled in the air, spinning and tumbling happily.

"GaK!"

A large, clawed hand grabbed the d'fly in a huge scaly fist. Goldie burst into sparkles and vanished.

"What do you think you're doing?!" Kara's temper flared red hot, her jewel pulsing dangerously inside her dress.

"I caught a fairy dragon," a massive lizard creature chuckled, revealing a long set of sharp teeth.

"That's *my* fairy dragon!"

"Fe, fi, fo, fum. I smell magic, gonna get me some." The giant creature advanced menacingly, making Kara cringe. Its thick neck and torso were covered in black leather studded with chrome buckles and spikes.

"I smell something worse." Another lizard monster loomed over her, blocking any escape. "A *human* with magic!"

A golden bubble popped behind Kara. Goldie walked up her shoulder, straightened her tux and stuck out her tongue.

"Who invited you here?" the first creature sneered, fanged smile shining wickedly.

"I did." The Forest Prince materialized from the crowd, smiling. His silver sword glittered dangerously in its sheath.

The creatures snarled, but stepped back.

The masked boy bowed. "My lady, would you do me the honor of a dance?"

"Totally," Kara breathed, grabbing his outstretched hand.

He led her onto the crowded dance floor, where disguised creatures of all shapes and sizes whirled, spinning and dancing among the flashing lights.

"Friends of yours?" Kara asked.

"Bulwoggles," the Forest Prince said, moving to the thudding beat.

"I thought fairies were all cute and sparkly." Kara stood checking out the crowd.

"They're not fairy. They're creatures that feed on darker magic, like werebeasts or demons."

"What do they want?" Kara asked.

"What do you think?" he nodded at the silver necklace around Kara's neck. "Ever since the web went wild, more and more creatures have come here searching for magic. They're the bad guys, not me."

"Everyone seems to think you steal magic too." Kara glared.

"A lot of stuff gets blamed on me. That's okay, as long as I can help those who need magic most."

"So, sometimes bad is good, huh," Kara commented.

Goldie was frolicking in milky moonbeams, sommersaulting with a small flying bear-like creature wearing a tutu and a pirate hat.

"Goldie's made a new friend," Kara said, watching the pair chattering up a storm.

"That's Spinnel, an evolved form of fairy dragon," the boy explained.

Kara regarded the strange assortment of creatures. It felt like they were all eyeing her, checking her out. It gave her the creeps. "Your note said I could help Lyra," she said adamantly. "Where is she?"

"In the goblin castle," he said spinning away. "But I really brought you here to convince you to go after the fire stallion."

"Ride it yourself," Kara said, annoyed. Had he

lured her here just for her magic? No way was Kara Davies putting up with that! She bolted.

"This is a rough crowd, don't go wander—Princess?" The Forest Prince stopped in mid turn, looking around. "Wait." He ran to her side, grabbing hold of her arm. "It's the only way to help Lyra."

Kara stopped short, cheeks flushed with anger, acutely aware of his fingers on her arm.

"She's at the goblin castle being treated by Tangoo," he said quickly, removing his hand. "But I don't trust him."

"Why should I trust you?" Kara asked suspiciously.

Green eyes shone from behind the black mask as he stared deep into Kara's eyes. "You are the blazing star. You defeated the Dark Sorceress."

Kara went rigid.

"But now she's working with two dark fairy creatures. One is an elemental magic master, the Spider Witch, the other is . . . something else."

Fear inched along Kara's spine. How much did he know about her real connection to the Dark Sorceress?

"I think they're working to escape the Otherworlds," he told her.

"And you know this how?"

"I work with the fairy underground, a secret group organized to fight them. According to our

information
have been p
creatures roa
supply." He look
Spider Witch had one of
foolishly used it to try and capture a her
unicorns."

"My friends and I stopped them," Kara said.

"Yes, you did." The boy's eyes twinkled in admiration. "Now they seek another one, here in the Fairy Realms. You have to find it first."

"The only thing *I* want," Kara said hotly, "is to help Lyra!"

The Forest Prince continued as if Kara hadn't spoken. "Rumor has it, the Spider Witch is going to attempt to reweave the web. Starting with the Fairy Realms."

"Is that even possible?" Kara couldn't picture it.

"The power crystals control the magic of Avalon itself. I'm not willing to take that risk, are you?"

Kara gulped. She had failed to ride the fire stallion. How was she supposed to find the crystal all by herself, with only Goldie to help her?

"We have to keep moving," the boy said, scanning a suspicious group that was pushing through the crowds. Kara recognized the yellow slitted eyes of bulwoggles as they locked on hers.

"We must leave before the stroke of midnight," he said worriedly, trying to find the exit.

"What ha ght, you turn into a pumpkin?" sh hen gulped. The bulwog-gles were ir way right toward them.

"What now, my man?"

The larg bulwoggle pushed masked dancers aside and stomped toward her. But before it had taken two steps, a red and green striped bunny-like creature with dragon wings flew in graceful figure eights around the lizard. Glimmering circles on the creature's body shimmered like a collection of magic gems.

"Out of my way, Elfan," the bulwoggle snarled.

"Let's Bulwoogie!" Elfan grabbed the bulwoggle and started dancing away.

Suddenly loud chimes echoed across the glade.

"We're too late!" the boy's voice held an edge of desperation.

"Fairies, trolls, and hobnobblers!" A voice broke over the speaker system. "Amaze your friends, shock your date, it's time to take off your masks and reveal your true identities!"

"I see," Kara smiled wickedly. "What's your rush?"

"On my count . . ." The DJ continued.

Giggles of excitement ran through the rave as the crowd eagerly prepared to take off their masks.

". . . one, two, go!"

Masks flew high in the air as dwarves, sprites, gnomes, and dozens of other fairy creatures revealed their own grinning faces.

"It's not much of a surprise anymore," Kara said, taking off her elaborate peacock mask, blinking ice blue eyes at the boy.

The Forest Prince gasped. "Only a fool would not be stunned each time he beheld your beauty."

Kara blushed. "Stop stalling. Your turn," she ordered.

He leaned in close and smiled.

Kara reached up and untied the black silk mask. His green eyes twinkled as she pulled it away.

"Hey!" she exclaimed.

He was wearing another black mask, exactly the same, underneath it.

Kara looked to Goldie, widening her blue eyes. The d'fly immediately understood Kara's thoughts and casually flew by the Forest Prince's shoulder. With one swift flap of her wing, Goldie snagged the second mask and ripped it off.

"You!" Kara gasped.

"You!" the bulwoggle sneered, towering over Kara.

"You!" Goldie squealed to the flying bunny.

"Hello," the bunny smiled.

The boy snatched the mask and turned away, quickly tying it around his face again.

It was the Goblin Prince, Lorren! But the handsome boy looked nothing like the primly dressed goblin she'd seen earlier that day in the Fairy Ring. 'Cept they both were green.

"What is going on?" Kara began, wondering what game Lorren was trying to play.

The bulwoggle chuckled, eyes flashing eagerly as it reached for Kara. The others appeared behind her, separating her from Lorren.

"Unhand that princess!" Lorren grabbed the bulwoggle and spun it around.

Razor teeth flashed as the creature roared, taking a swipe at the boy with a massive fist.

Lorren easily dodged the blow. He turned, giving the creature a kick in the rear, sending it flying. But the others were on him, locking his arms behind his back. The first bulwoggle towered over the boy, ready to rip his head off.

"Let him go!" Kara commanded.

Lorren and the bulwoggles stopped.

The blazing star stood, arm raised. In her hand, the diamond-white unicorn jewel pulsed with power.

Lorren groaned. "Oh great."

The bulwoggles' eyes flashed with hunger.

Kara held her gem with trembling fingers. *Uh oh, maybe this wasn't such a good idea,* she thought, surveying the mass of magic starved creatures around her.

"It's only a girl," the bulwoggle taunted.

Kara felt the hot rush of power flowing through her as the jewel erupted with blazing white magic. The bulwoggle howled as its angry companions dove out of the way.

"Kaaraaa!" Goldie's claws dug into her shoulder.

The d'fly's voice snapped Kara back to reality. She had to get control of her magic before she lost herself completely in the swirling brilliance of her own power. Screaming with the effort, she wrenched the magic back.

The crowd of costumed creatures stared at her in shocked silence.

A cluster of fairies zipped above her head, forming a bright blue spotlight. Her jewel pulsed, draping her in shards of sparkling diamond magic.

"She's got a jewel!"

"Magic!"

"It's the blazing star!" squeaked a pixie, hopping so excitedly her pickle costume fell off.

Costumed creatures shoved and pushed each other, everyone trying to nose in and get a good look at Kara and her magic. The Forest Prince began ushering her to the door. A riot was about to break out.

"Take a picture!" Kara cried, holding up the sparking gem. "It'll last longer."

Jagged lighting split the skies over the isle as clouds swirled. A gust of wind howled through the rave. Discarded masks skittered across the floor and fairy lanterns bobbed in midair.

Something flew from the clouds, spinning like a whirlpool. It glided down, skimming over the heads of the crowd. Partygoers yelled and cheered. The swirling light came to a stop and landed right in front of Kara, expanding as it spun in rainbow spirals. This was no light show. It was a portal.

"Kara!" Emily's voice echoed through the portal. "Can you hear me?"

"Emily!"

"Jump through," Emily screamed.

The portal followed Kara as she turned and moved away.

"Not without Lyra!" Kara yelled, backing away from the snarling bulwoggles.

"This might be your only chance," the healer's voice echoed desperately. "Tweek doesn't know if it will open again!"

"Give me the magic!" the bulwoggle leader roared, his crazed eyes locked on Kara's jewel.

"Stay away from me!" Kara shrieked.

"What?!" Emily asked, startled.

"Not you, the bulwoggle!"

"Bulwoggle?!" Ozzie screamed from the other side of the portal.

The bulwoggle lunged, huge muscled arms outstretched.

"Stay back," Lorren yelled. Sword in his hand, he took on all three bulwoggles, trying to keep them from Kara.

Something rattled in Kara's purse.

"I gotta go. I have a situation."

The bag burst open and Mirabelle flew out. "I

couldn't stay away, let me reflect your radiant beauty—*arkq!*"

A giant clawed hand swiped at the clamshell mirror sending her spinning as Puffdoggie sprang out. It hit the bulwoggle in the nose with an explosion of twinkly puff powder.

"AhhHHH ChOOOO!"

Mirabelle, Puffdoggie, and Goldie tumbled head over heels as the bulwoggle staggered backwards.

"Oh no!" Kara watched in horror—as the vicious lizard creature fell into the swirling portal and vanished.

Kara waved her arms, trying to swat the portal away from the dance floor. The portal veered crazily on its axis and dove sharply into the screaming crowd. Three more creatures were sucked in before she could send it airborne again.

"We have to get out of here before the entire rave falls through!" Lorren yelled.

"Whooo! This rocks, dude!" A dwarf whirled skyward and vanished into the portal.

"Let's get out of here!" Lorren yelled.

Stuffing Mirabelle and Puffdoggie in her purse, Kara grabbed Goldie and ran after the prince. The portal followed, zipping overhead.

Troves of trolls dove out of the way, overturning the food stands

Together, princess, prince, and dragonfly charged through the mists and out of the archway, skidding down to the water's edge.

Hordes of enraged creatures poured from the archways, chasing them.

"You sure know how to show a girl a good time," Kara commented.

"Thank you." Lorren let out a piercing whistle.

With a whoosh of giant wings, the goblin bat swooped out of the night. The crowd ducked and rolled to avoid the huge wings. A clipped bulwoggle went flying face first into the muddy bank. Lorren took a running leap, grabbed hold of the saddle and hauled himself up.

Lorren reached out his hand. "Shall we escape?"

Kara hesitated. Her new friend was not only an outlaw, but also a goblin. But bandit or not, she had to trust someone.

Grabbing Lorren's hand, she swung into the saddle behind him. In a flash, the bat was airborne, the Fairy Isle shrinking far below. The portal followed, zipping into the sky, trailing after them.

"Emily!" Kara squashed Goldie to her ear. "Come in, Emily!"

But all she heard was screaming, crashing, and the sounds of her room being completely trashed.

Chapter 8

The spinning portal shimmered and glowed like a small sun in Kara's closet. Everyone had stepped away, huddled in the center of the room except—

"The portal's opened!"

Musso and Sparky barreled for the bright circle.

"Incoming corporeal particles transporting across the astral planes!" Tweek announced, focusing his jewel like a magnifying glass at the edges of the swirling hole.

"What?" Musso asked, running by the little twig figure.

"Something is coming thr—*aaArgghk!*"

A mass of scaly muscles crashed through the portal, sending Musso and Sparky flying back into the bedroom.

Roaring with fury, the bulwoggle destroyed a row of Kara's summer dresses with one deadly sweep of its claws.

"A bulwoggle!" Musso cried, crawling onto the

windowsill, fumbling with his utility belt to free a few spells. "Mercenaries! The war has started!"

Tearing a pile of pink sweaters off its head, the lizard creature stomped into the bedroom. "What place is this?" it bellowed.

"Go back!" Adriane yelled, as she and Dreamer stepped in front of their friends. "You don't belong here!"

Yellow slitted eyes moved from the snarling black mistwolf to the golden magic sparking from the warrior's wolf stone.

"I will take that magic!" it bellowed, eyes shining wide.

Adriane spun and kicked the closet door closed. Twisted hangers shot from the closet as the beast smashed the door back open, crushing Tweek into a mass of moss and twigs.

Ozzie dove under the bed as Spinnel suddenly barreled out of the portal, smacking into the back of the bulwoggle's head.

Trying to pry the bear creature loose, the bulwoggle rampaged across Kara's room, wreaking havoc.

Dreamer leaped, locking teeth into the monster's leather armor, spinning around the room in a wide circle. He crashed into Musso, sending the hobgoblin's fistful of spells flying. Magic splattered against the shelves, covering two stuffed bears, a hippo, and a moose. The stuffed animals twirled to the ground in a fluffy tangle of limbs just as a flailing dwarf flew from the portal and crashed through the canopy of Kara's bed.

"Whoa, dude! Is this the VIP room?" the dwarf hung upside down as the ripped material caught his feet.

"I will swallow your magic, and you with it!" the bulwoggle roared.

"Eat this!" Adriane yelled, Dreamer at her side, Fred and Fiona on one shoulder, Barney and Blaze on the other, lending their magic to her intense golden fire.

"Beeeeat it!" the d'flies chorused.

Golden wolf fire slammed the beast right in its armored chest. The bulwoggle tottered and fell across the bed, bringing the canopy down with it. The bedspring collapsed, and the bed crashed to the floor.

"Hey, keep it down up there!" Mrs. Davies's annoyed voice floated up the stairs.

A screaming bunny with dragon wings hurtled from the portal and bowled Ozzie into Kara's stereo, sending CDs flying.

"Sorry!" Emily answered Mrs. Davies, her stone glowing bright blue as she grabbed Ozzie out of the way of Elfan. "Just helping Kara rehearse!"

A red, yellow, and blue fox dressed like Robin

Hood in green tights and cape stepped from the closet and bowed. "Cotax, fairy underground. May I be of some assistance?"

"What is this, a convention?" Ozzie exclaimed, sliding across the floor on loose CD cases.

"Roll it up in the quilt!" Adriane commanded.

The mages, Ozzie, the d'flies, Dreamer, Spinnel, Elfan, Cotax, and Kara's stuffed animals all jumped on the roiling lump entangled in the large quilt.

"Your friend has caused quite a scene at the rave." Cotax smiled, holding down the monster's thrashing tail.

"Leave it to Kara to find a party," Adriane commented as she and the others lugged the rolled-up creature back toward the closet.

"Give me that magic!" The bulwoggle mumbled, now wrapped like a mummy in Kara's quilt.

"The portal's shrinking!" Tweek yelled, sticking his flattened twiggy head dangerously close to the flashing circle.

Together, the group heaved the screaming quilt into the closet.

The bulwoggle fell into the portal, Kara's blouses and sweaters tangled on flailing scaly limbs.

"Hurry!" Emily shouted, herding the fairy creatures toward Kara's closet.

Elfan, Cotax, and Spinnel dove through, the dwarf charging behind.

"Thanks for the party, dudes."

Sparky ran at top speed, Musso right on his heels.

But just as the dwarf disappeared, the portal shuddered and vanished.

"Gaahdoooff!" Sparky and Musso hurtled through the suddenly empty space and smashed nose first into the back of Kara's closet.

"I see stars . . . ," Musso said dreamily, sliding down the wall into a heap.

"Tha webbbb ith bootifull," Sparky slurred, and collapsed nose first to the floor.

"Tweek, is it going to open again?" Adriane asked anxiously.

Everyone gathered around the little Fairimental as he raised his turquoise gemstone and scanned the closet. After a tense moment of silence, he smiled broadly.

"No problem," the EF said, riffling through holographic numerals. "It should open again in about three years!"

* * *

Lorren's gloved hand gently clasped Kara's as she slid from the bat's saddle into the fairy palace bedroom window.

"Thanks for a great time!" She tossed her bag onto the dresser.

"Hmph!" Goldie snorted, then flew into the room, shaking off her costume.

"Hey, it could have been worse. We could still be

raining fairy creatures all over the kingdoms," Lorren quipped.

"And my Capris with them!" Kara turned her eyes down. "I'm sorry. I didn't know that portal would follow me."

"Hey, I'm sorry, too," Lorren said, then paused. "If I'd known the rave was going to be so dangerous, I never would have asked you there."

"At least it wasn't boring," she answered, smiling, but then frowned as she looked up into his masked face. "Prince Lorren, or whatever I should call you."

He touched the edge of his mask absently. "The Fairy Realms are in real trouble. I can't work with the underground if everyone knows who I am," he explained, then smiled. "Besides, my parents would lock me in the dungeon if they knew what I was doing."

"Maybe your parents would like the Forest Prince," Kara suggested.

"Were yours thrilled when you told them you were a mage?" he countered.

"Well, I, um, I see your point," Kara stammered. None of the mages had told anyone—who'd believe them?

Lorren nodded. "Ironic, isn't it? I have to hide who I am so I can be myself. You should understand my secret better than anybody, blazing star."

Kara gazed into his pale green eyes with new understanding.

"Look, I have no right to ask you, but if you still want to go after the fire stallion, I can take you to Tangoo," he said, gathering the bat's reins.

"But you said you didn't trust him."

"It was his idea to combine the blazing star with a firemental horse to attract the power crystal. If anyone knows how to find the fire stallion, it'll be he." He looked at her, waiting.

Kara wondered if she should trust Lorren. It was all so confusing. But if he'd wanted to hurt her, he could have left her to the bulwoggles. Instead, he'd risked himself to save her. And if he had secret-identity issues, well, so did she.

The boy turned away, bowed his head, and raised the reins, about to fly off.

"Lorren," Kara called out as the bat moved away from her window.

"Yes, Princess?" He turned, his face a silhouette rimmed in starlight.

"See you tomorrow."

Kara watched him glide over the gardens until the darkness swallowed him.

"He's cute!" Skirmish broke the silence, clattering across the vanity table.

Kara's purse wiggled and fell open. Mirabelle flopped open on the dresser. "What a party!"

Puffdoggie burst out barking, sprinkling powder over Angelo.

"This is completely against regulations!" the comb cried to the stowaways. "You really rattle my teeth!"

"They were a big help," Kara called as she walked from the bathroom, wrapping the fluffy robe around her.

"Well?" Whiffle asked Kara, huffing a cloud of lilac. "Details, we need details."

Kara flopped onto the bed, exhausted. "Bulwoggles, flying bunnies, riots, random portals, secret identities—everything a girl could want."

"Oooo!" Skirmish shouted, leaping up to brush out Kara's hair. "How were the snacks?"

"Shhh, Skirmish, can't you see she's tired?" Mirabelle scolded.

Kara sunk into the big pillow. Tomorrow she would visit the Goblin Castle and Tangoo. But what if Lorren was wrong? What if the sorcerer couldn't help? Lyra would melt into nothing, all because Kara couldn't control her magic. Then she'd be trapped and alone in the Fairy Realms, in the middle of a war that could destroy everything she loved. Even if by some remote chance she found the fire stallion, how could she bond with it? Her magic sure didn't work last time. And how could she possibly find the power crystal? What if the Dark Sorceress got her hands on it first! Hot tears stung her eyes. Why was all this resting on her shoulders? If only she'd never had magic in the first place, this never would have happened.

Goldie nuzzled into Kara's neck.

"Goldie, can you call Fiona?" Kara asked, petting the d'fly's soft, golden hide.

The mini settled next to Kara's ear and sent a series of squeaks to Fiona.

"Kara?" Emily's voice asked.

"Hi," Kara sniffled. "Anyone miss me?"

"Everyone. How are you?" Emily asked.

"I dunno," Kara answered quietly. "How's my room?"

"Well, Blaze and Barney are redecorating, but everything's quiet, finally. Ozzie took Musso and Sparky to Ravenswood for the night—"

"I messed up so bad," Kara cried, words suddenly pouring out. "If I lose Lyra, I don't know what I'll do. I'm not strong like Adriane. And the fire stallion hated me. I don't know what to do!"

"Kara," Emily said gently. "You can't change what happened. There's so much we don't know about our magic."

"Yeah, but your magic *works*. I don't know what mine is supposed to do, except make a giant disaster out of everything. I wish I didn't have it at all!" Kara started sobbing.

The enchanted accessories clambered onto the bed, trying to calm the princess, brushing and spritzing everywhere.

"Your magic is part of you now, Kara," Emily said. "Wishing you didn't have it is like wishing you weren't yourself. We all know there's only one Kara, and that's the way we like it."

Kara hiccupped a bit of laughter. "Guess I'm stuck with me no matter what."

A strange beeping noise blared from Goldie.

"Hold on, call waiting," Kara said. She poked Goldie's belly, making the d'fly giggle.

"Kara, are you there?" Adriane's voice asked worriedly.

"Hey."

"How you doing?"

"Better, thanks, I'm on the other line with Emily," Kara said. "Let me see if we can do a conference call."

Goldie gurgled, and Kara heard the other two mages talking through their dragonfly phones.

"I'm glad you called, Adriane," Kara said.

"Where did all those creatures come from?" the warrior asked.

"Long story short, I went to a fairy rave with the masked mystery guy," Kara said. "The portal followed me. "And guess what else?" Kara rolled onto her stomach, propping herself on her elbows, knees bent, feet in the air.

"What?" Emily asked.

"He's really the Goblin Prince Lorren in disguise!"

"No way!" Emily and Adriane chorused.

"Totally."

Emily giggled. "You're dating a goblin!"

"Somebody get Mrs. Davies a Valium," Adriane said.

"And get this, Lorren is totally cute!" Kara exclaimed, then felt herself blushing. "I mean, he's like, different from other goblins we've seen."

"No warts?" Adriane asked.

"No." Kara paused, feeling a sudden smile spread over her face. "He's just like a real boy."

"So what if he happens to be green," Adriane added.

"Yeah, so, anyway," Kara continued seriously. "I have to find the power crystal to save Lyra."

"And you need the fire stallion to get the crystal?" Emily asked.

"Yeah, Lorren thinks this goblin sorcerer can help me find the horse. Supposedly the combination of our magic will draw the power crystal to me."

"Magic attracts magic," Emily concluded.

"What if I can't . . ." Kara's words faded.

"Listen to me, Kara," Adriane said firmly. "You're not going to lose Lyra. Okay?"

Kara sniffled again. "Okay."

"We'll cover for you tomorrow at the play," Emily reminded Kara.

"I totally forgot! Someone is bound to notice me missing."

"We'll figure it out," Emily assured her. "Get some rest. Fiona and Fred are here if you need us."

"Okay, guys. Thanks."

Kara lifted Goldie from her ear, breaking the connection. She hugged the d'fly close, clinging to the words of her friends and the strength of their magic.

Chapter 9

Kara stood in the bright morning sunlight, Goldie on her shoulder, taking in the expansive Fairy Gardens. Elaborate pathways wound through, fountains, gazebos, and floating fairy bridges. But here and there delicate flowers were fading, their once vibrant colors washed and pale, leaving a feeling of emptiness throughout the gardens.

The golden sun felt too hot, and Kara removed her dark blue jacket trimmed with white fleece, tucking it under her arm. She'd chosen a very fashionable riding outfit from the closet this morning, complete with tan suede riding pants tucked into knee-high leather boots and a white silk blouse. Her long blond hair was pulled back into a ponytail, her unicorn jewel blazing on its necklace against her tan skin.

Goldie squeaked and pointed.

In the distance Kara saw what looked like a rainbow cloud sweeping over the gardens. It was dragonflies, dozens of them in every conceivable color, leaving sparkling trails like miniature crop dusters.

Goldie squeaked and pointed.

"That's an amazing fairy dragon you have."

Kara turned to see Queen Selinda approach, regal in a flowing golden gown. She gave Kara a smile. "I've never seen one bond with anyone. They are usually so independent."

"Goldie's special," Kara said, scritching between the mini's ears.

"As is her bonded." Selinda smiled.

"What's happening here?"" Kara asked as they walked under a purple and white willow whose branches drooped with withering leaves.

Selinda sighed. "Not even the fairy dragons can keep the gardens alive. The heart of the magic is fading."

"But if magic is flowing wild everywhere else, why is it fading here?" Kara asked.

"That is precisely why. Avalon's magic should flow here first, then to the web, and then to all other worlds. But now that's not happening."

Kara looked at the gardens. "Then this is all my fault, too."

"Aldenmor would have perished if you had not released the magic of Avalon," the queen explained. "You did what was needed."

"I messed up, as usual." Kara's eyes were brimming with tears. "Look what I did to Lyra."

Selinda wiped slender fingers across Kara's face, drying her tears. "We don't really know what happened, do we?"

"I . . ." Kara replayed the moment in her mind. She'd been using her jewel and something had gone wrong. Her magic had reflected off a mirror and hit Lyra. "So maybe that wasn't my fault?" Kara asked, mulling over the possibility. Could the mirror have altered her magic?

"I don't know, Kara. But I do know that humans who bond with magical animals make the most formidable magic users."

"I didn't do so well with that horse," Kara reminded the queen.

"It's a Firemental," Selinda said, as if that explained everything. "A very bold plan from Tangoo. Some might even say desperate."

Looking out over the grand gardens, she continued. "Magic is our most precious resource, part of a delicate ecosystem connecting us to the web and all other worlds. Each of the kingdoms and all the different fairies and fairy creatures that live here help to make magic stronger."

"Even the goblins?" Kara asked, trying to imagine the hot-tempered Goblin Queen spreading magic for the good of the worlds.

Selinda's fine features tensed. "The goblins and fairies have had their differences, but they have been terribly manipulated by the Dark Sorceress. I know Raelda wants the best for her kingdom, and I would like to think we could become friends. But if we have to go to war to save the Fairy Realms, we will."

Kara thought of Lorren. Was she his friend or his enemy? Whose side was *she* on, anyway?

Seeing Kara's troubled expression, the queen fell silent for a moment as they walked toward the Fairy Ring.

"I heard there was quite a party last night on the Fairy Isle." The queen raised an eyebrow, a twinkle in her eye.

Kara gave the queen a quick glance. "I, um . . ."

"Angelo filled me in." The queen smiled.

Kara frowned. Ooh, that big mouth comb!

"Fairy raves are very much a part of us," Selinda explained. "Music, dancing, and creative expression are what we live for. Although in these times, raves can be dangerous."

Kara glanced at the queen. "I'm sorry I snuck out."

"Evidently you had good company."

"He's not what he seems," Kara said quickly.

"Now that's your fairy blood speaking," Selinda chuckled softly. "Many things are not what they seem in the Fairy Realms."

"Wait, how can I be part fairy? Does that mean my family is, too?"

Selinda shook her head. "Fairy blood skips human generations but is particularly strong in you. You are directly descended from Queen Lucinda, the greatest of all Fairy Queens."

"Tell me about her," Kara asked.

"She was a great leader, a blazing star. She truly believed in the goodness and magic of all living things."

"What happened to her?"

"She had a sister."

Kara stiffened. The Dark Sorceress.

They walked into the empty Fairy Ring, heading through archways of yellow and red flowers swaying gently in the breeze.

Selinda smiled, her violet eyes searching Kara's troubled expression.

"I wish I had all the answers for you, Kara. In a few hours, this ring will be filled again with the kings and queens from the other kingdoms and we must decide the future of the Fairy Realms. And perhaps the future of the web itself."

Kara looked in Selinda's eyes. They were full of compassion.

"You do not have to stay here against your will.." The queen paused. "You have a legacy of great goodness, and also of darkness. But your path is your own."

Kara steeled herself. There was only one path for her right now. "Queen Selinda, I'm going to save Lyra."

"Then you must go to the goblins."Queen Selinda waved her hand to the grand mirror by her throne. ""You *are* the one we've been waiting for. Be strong and proud of who you are."

"Thank you. I will." Kara stepped to the mirror and held up her jewel. It blazed with the mighty power of the unicorns. The image swirled, spreading like circles in a stream. Kara put her hand up and slipped it through the glass. Before she could change her mind, she stepped through and vanished.

❁ ❁ ❁

On the other side of the mirror, Kara found herself in a bustling courtyard in the center of a huge castle. Towering walls surrounded her. She looked over the ramparts and gasped. The enormous castle was built of gleaming gray stone, perched on a cliff overlooking amazing waterfalls that plunged straight down into clouds of white foam. In the distance the landscape was covered with thick forests, deep blue lakes, and gray boulders that lay on surging green hills like sleeping giants.

"Good morning, Princess." Lorren ran to greet her, his voice slightly high and nasal. "Welcome to Castle Garthwyn!" he said proudly, smoothing his deep blue tunic. Sweeping his velvet cap from his head, he bowed deeply. Spiky black hair with green highlights stuck out over pointy ears.

Lorren the Goblin Prince was nothing like Lorren the Forest Prince. A gleam in his green eyes was Kara's only hint of the dashing outlaw in black she had come to know. But which was the real Lorren?

"Lorren!" a loud voice echoed throughout the courtyard.

He tensed, turning toward his mother, Queen Raelda, who charged down the castle's steps, looking angry as a thundercloud.

"Is this any way to welcome the princess!" the stout green woman demanded. "Princess Kara, we are honored to have you here." Raelda curtsied formally, making Kara uneasy.

"The honor is mine, your highness," Kara returned with a bow, not knowing what else to do.

"So, you have decided to continue on your quest." Raelda guided Kara up the grand stone steps leading to the castle's enormous wooden doors. Crystal torches lit the cavernous entryway.

"Yes, ma'am."

"Good, good, you have guts. I like guts."

Goblins paused in their duties to nod respectfully to their queen, some even smiling shyly at the blazing star. Kara smiled back, amazed. She didn't feel anything but curiosity from the Goblin folk here.

"Terrible business with that horse," Raelda fretted.

"Frankly we had our doubts Tangoo could pull this off. Firementals are so unpredictable."

"Queen Raelda, thank you for helping Lyra," Kara said to the queen. "She means more to me than anything. I'm very grateful to you."

Raelda's eyes softened. "I am familiar with familiars." She eyed Goldie, raising an eyebrow as the fairy dragon grinned. "The fact that you are here, ready to keep trying, shows me what you are truly made of, Princess."

She stopped and looked Kara directly in the eye. "But make no mistake. I will do what I must to save my kingdom." Then she turned and walked away. "Good luck. May the magic be with you."

"This way, Princess." Lorren led Kara to an elevator door on the right end of the entry hall. "Impressive, you did good," he said, smiling.

"You think?"

"You're still here." Lorren whisked Kara into the elevator and pulled the winch. Gears turned noisily as the car rose.

"How is Lyra?" Kara asked.

"I won't lie to you," Lorren said slowly, as the elevator rose up the tower. "You had better prepare yourself."

Kara swallowed the lump in her throat.

The elevator opened before a large bronze door.

"Welcome to the goblin laboratory, Princess," he said, flinging the door wide.

Kara stared in amazement at the incredible round room. A domed ceiling flooded light through several skylights. Shelves built into the stone walls held countless vials and bottles of colored liquids. Metal instruments, scales, and mysterious twisted objects were scattered about next to smoking cauldrons. Along one section of rounded wall, sunlight reflected off dozens of immense magic mirrors at least fifteen feet high, dazzling Kara's eyes.

Something clattered among a pile of crystals and lenses. "Lorren!" a girl's voice said. "You've got to see this!"

Blinking away the mirror's light, Kara saw a young goblin girl rising from the far side of a wooden table. Her skin was light green, and she wore a long smock covered in splotches of colors. She lifted a pair of protective goggles back onto hair black as midnight, pulled into a tight bun. She had been working on a strange hand mirror whose silver frame was adorned with two metal antennae. "Oh." She stopped when she saw Kara. Her green skin blushed purple.

"Princess Kara, this is Tasha, Tangoo's assistant," Lorren said.

Goldie squeaked, insulted.

"And Goldie, the wonder dragon," he added.

Tasha bent into a low, clumsy bow and stammered, "An honor, your magnificent, wonder highness."

"Please, just call me Kara," she said, and smiled. The goblin girl seemed about her age, Kara noticed. "It's nice to meet you."

Tasha stood, self-consciously wiping the smudges from her smock.

"Look at all these spells Tasha made all by herself," Lorren proclaimed, proudly pointing to a rack of shelves neatly stacked with labeled vials. "What are you working on now, a love spell?" he teased.

Tasha flushed purple again. "I finished those in my first year of training."

"Ah, those things never work, anyway," Lorren said, and laughed.

"How would you know?" Tasha asked slyly.

"Funny. Where's Tangoo?" Lorren surveyed the cluttered laboratory.

"He's checking the mirrors for the princess's ride," the goblin girl said, and looked to Kara. "I'm so sorry about your friend. I've been keeping her as cool as possible." Tasha gestured to an enormous tank sunken into the floor. It was filled with a pool of shimmering quicksilver, with a strange lump in the middle. Kara gasped. The lump was Lyra's head and broad shoulders! The cat's blurred features were a melted mockery of her once beautiful face.

"Lyra," she sobbed, kneeling by the tank. She didn't need a sorcerer to tell her that Lyra's time was running out fast.

"Yes, it certainly is a shame," a cool voice echoed across the room.

The trio whirled around, startled to find Tangoo standing right behind them.

"Master Tangoo!" Tasha cried.

"Tangoo, Princess Kara is here!" Lorren pointed.

"I can see that, Prince Lorren." The sorcerer smiled thinly, looking down his hawk nose at Kara. "Princess, you did not fare so well with the Firemental horse."

That's an understatement, thought Kara.

"But, I am happy to say, you look ready to ride now," he continued.

"If I get the crystal, can it save Lyra?" Kara asked anxiously.

"The crystal of Avalon certainly has the power to bring the cat back," Tangoo assured her.

"If her unicorn jewel enchanted the cat in the first place, why can't the princess undo the spell herself?" Lorren asked suspiciously.

Yeah, why hadn't she thought of that? Kara asked herself.

Tangoo's sharp eyes darkened. "Well, my obstinate yet positive young prince, if the princess were a magic master, that *might* be possible, otherwise"—he waved his long fingers—"Good-bye kitty." The old sorcerer smiled thinly.

Lorren's brow furrowed.

Kara's heart sank as she fought to stay strong. "How can I find the stallion?"

"It will not be easy," the sorcerer warned. "Firementals are most difficult to harness. That spell took months to conjure. But it cannot hold. The creature will dissolve back to fire."

"Oh no! How long have we got?" Kara asked, frightened.

"The horse may have already reverted to fire." He tapped his goatee with a slender, green finger. "However, if you were to find the Blue Rose, that would give the Firemental enough magic to stay in its stallion form, long enough for you to ride the mirrors."

"The Blue Rose! An ancient talisman that holds powerful elemental magic!" Tasha cried, reciting her schooling perfectly.

"Quite right, my eager-eared apprentice," Tangoo smiled.

Tasha beamed.

"The Blue Rose is a myth!" Lorren said dismissively. "Everyone knows that."

"I beg to differ, my inexperienced but pigheaded prince," Tangoo countered. "I know where it is hidden."

"Where?" all three asked.

"In the lair of the Spider Witch."

Kara frowned. That didn't sound good at all.

"Oh, don't worry, Princess," Tasha reassured her.

"The Spider Witch is locked away in the fairy prisons known as the Otherworlds."

"The Blue Rose fuels elemental magic," Tangoo continued. "If you were to get the rose, the horse would come to you. It is the only way for it to survive."

"How do you know all this?" Lorren asked.

The sorcerer arched an eyebrow. Kara caught a spark of anger in his eyes, but it dimmed quickly. "My plucky but pimply prince, I was an expert in elemental magic long before you were a little goblet."

"But you'll have to be careful!" Tasha told Kara, her pointy ears twitching. "The Blue Rose is entwined on the same vine with an identical rose, which is extremely deadly to elemental magic."

"How do I tell them apart?" Kara asked.

"The Fairy Rhyme—every young sorcerer learns it in Spellology 101." Tasha cleared her throat and chanted, "The roses are blue, but only one can be true. The flower with the power is the bloom with the fume. The bud that's a dud seems a rose to the nose. Get it?"

"Got it," Kara affirmed.

"Good."

Tangoo smiled. "I have located a mirror in the Spider Witch's castle."

"Are you sure about this?" Lorren asked. "The Spider Witch might have left traps."

"These are dangerous times," the sorcerer replied.

"I'm going with her," Lorren declared.

"Prince Lorren." Tangoo's thin lips stretched into a frown as he studied the prince and the sword strapped to his side. "I thought you hated mirror jumping."

"I . . . uh . . . I'll live."

"Yes, astral plane jumping can turn one's stomach." Tangoo tapped his goatee thoughtfully. "I think I have something that will make the jump a bit less disorienting."

"Okay, let's do it." Kara nodded.

"Tasha," Tangoo said, handing her a slip of parchment, "prepare a mirror with these coordinates."

"Yes, Master Tangoo." Tasha walked up to a sleek gray mirror. She adjusted nearly invisible knobs and buttons along its edges.

Like a little hawk, Goldie watched the tall sorcerer reach a long-fingered hand up to a row of vials.

"Thanks, Tasha," Lorren said.

Tasha blushed. "All ready."

"See you on the other side," Lorren said to Kara.

Tangoo walked to Lorren. "I think you'll really *love* this spell, Prince Lorren," the sorcerer chuckled.

Twinkly magic flew from the sorcerer's outstretched hands.

Goldie squawked and leaped, intercepting the spell meant for Lorren. A bright flash surrounded Goldie, knocking the d'fly off balance and sending the mini plummeting through the mirror.

"Goldie!" Kara screamed, flashing on Lyra's horrible enchantment.

She reached out to grab the mini and fell head over heels into the mirror's murky blackness.

Chapter 10

"This is never going to work." Adriane stood backstage in the school auditorium, looking uncertainly at Emily.

A blond wig adorned with a sparkling tiara covered Adriane's black hair. Her usual jeans and pullover had been replaced by a pink dress that poofed out in a mass of shining taffeta.

Emily tried to keep a straight face as she straightened the tiara. "You look like Tinkerbell."

"Pinkerbell," Ozzie corrected, polishing his ferret stone with the hem of Adriane's dress.

"She owes me big time for this!" Adriane groused, stomping her black hiking boots to straighten the dress.

"All you have to do is read this part." Emily pointed to the Fairy Queen Titania's lines. "Ozzie's magic will do the rest."

"Blah." Fred leaned over Adriane's puffy pink shoulder, head drooped.

"I agree," Adriane said, then noticed that Fred's

usually bright blue eyes were dulled and listless. "Hey, what's wrong, Fred?"

"Tummeee, Adriee," the blue mini complained.

Fiona's, Barney's, and Blaze's little heads lolled out of Emily's backpack.

"Aw, you guys eat something that upset your tummies?" Emily gently ran her rainbow gem over the dragonflies.

Four little heads nodded.

"Bad spell," Musso pronounced, looking into Fiona's half-closed eyes.

"What?" Emily said.

"They absorbed a bad spell. I ate an ice-cream spell once. It was so sweet, I passed out."

"What did you do now, Musso?" Adriane demanded.

"It wasn't me," Musso protested.

Fiona flapped her ruby wings. "Goldeee."

"Goldie sent the spell?" Emily placed her ear to Fiona's belly. It rumbled like a backfiring car.

"Forsooth, it's time for the costume check!" Rae hollered from center stage, clapping her hands. Student actors scurried onstage and lined up, straightening togas, wings and crowns.

Adriane shot a significant look to Ozzie. "Show-time."

Ozzie nodded and concentrated on his glowing golden ferret stone.

"Testing, one, two, pink shoe—" Adriane spoke—in Kara's voice!

Ozzie smiled. "Not bad! A ventriloquist mage."

Kyle ambled by, wearing a green-feathered Robin Hood hat and clutching his Shakespearean insult book. His eyes fell on Adriane and widened. "Thou reeky, plume-plucked pignut of a sister! I didn't see you leave for school this morning!"

"Be gone, flap-mouthed varlot!" Adriane bellowed, her voice a deep bass tone.

"Gah!" Ozzie sputtered. "Needs some minor magical modulation." He shook the stone and scrunched his whiskers in concentration.

"All hail the drama queen." Kyle strolled onstage, narrowly avoiding Rae. The director charged into the Fairy Ring set, tugging on a chartreuse velvet gown, her Shakespeare Day costume.

Backstage, Fiona's red hide flashed as Blaze's orange body started blinking brightly.

"I'll keep an eye on the d'flies," Emily reassured Adriane.

"Here goes." The warrior grimaced and stepped onstage, nearly running into Heather, Molly, and Tiffany as they scurried by, making some last-minute adjustments to their sparkling makeup and glittering costumes.

"K, why didn't you pick up your phone last night?" Tiffany demanded. "We were totally worried about you."

The warrior's voice came out squeaky and high pitched. "I, like, needed my beauty rest." Adriane sent an irritated look to Ozzie.

"I *love* your color contacts!" Molly grinned, looking into Adriane's dark eyes.

"If you ask me, everyone is acting weird," Heather exclaimed.

"HeeHawhello, ladies!" Marcus shuffled by, combing his donkey ears.

Rae marched back onstage, critically eyeing her actors' costumes. Her steely eyes bugged out when she saw Adriane. "Our Fairy Queen hath returned, and in a new dress!"

"Yeah, K, why'd you ditch the old costume?" Tiffany asked.

"It, like, totally wasn't pink enough," Adriane hissed in a voice like Darth Vader. She glared daggers offstage. "Excuse me," she peeped like a chipmunk, and stomped toward the ferret.

"Gak!" In the shadows offstage, Ozzie smacked his ferret stone furiously. "Er, Emily, I could use some help here."

But Emily's attention was on Barney, who suddenly shuddered in her arms.

"Fred, are you all right?" Adriane forgot the flabbergasted ferret as she held Fred.

The blue dragonfly belched like a trombone, barfing magic all over Adriane and covering her with sprinkly twinkles.

"Scooz meme." Fred dove into Emily's backpack, feeling better.

The warrior's eyes went hazy as she tottered and knocked into Marcus.

"Heew, you're all blue!"

Blue light surrounded the warrior in a shimmering halo as she gazed at the dreamy donkey.

"People, people, what is going on now?" Rae cried, marching over to look at Adriane's glowing head.

"BLaaaPHHHf." Fiona suddenly tumbled in the air and hurled, sending azure twinkles smacking into Rae's frizzy head. Rae careened backwards and fell onto Kyle.

"People, some professionalism, please!" Rae's eyes glazed over as she tried to disentangle herself from the sandy-haired boy. "Ooo, baby!" She stared at Kyle, a giddy smile suddenly plastered on her face.

"Whoa!" Kyle jumped to his feet and stumbled away from Rae.

"Come back, thou dreamiest of hunks!" the director cried. "Let me pledge my eternal love!"

"Kara, what is with you?!" The fairies shuttled over.

"BLrrrAAAFFF!" Barney and Blaze both tossed up the magic spell.

Molly, Tiffany, and Heather shrieked as clouds of twinkly bits covered them in a dazzling shower of popping lights.

"The dragons picked up a love bug." Musso observed Heather, Tiffany, and Molly, their eyes glazed over in ecstasy. "Those fairies will fall in love with the first—oop."

The three girls were advancing straight toward Musso, their shining eyes locked on him.

"Those are the cutest ears I ever saw! He's so *totally* cute. I saw him first. No way!"

"Ak!"

"Oh, no." Emily frantically stuffed the d'flies in her backpack before anyone saw them. She tried to catch Adriane's eye, but the warrior was completely ignoring her. Adriane's total attention was riveted on a very confused donkey. Marcus shuffled across stage, Adriane draped over him like a cloak.

"Don't ever leave me, my hairy Romeo."

The four minis peeked out from Emily's backpack as students started filing into the auditorium for the performance.

"Help!" Kyle yelled, Rae chasing him.

"Help!" Musso ran the other way, three fairies bounding and leaping after him.

"Heehawwwelp!" Marcus ran into the auditorium, plowing through crowds of students. Adriane hurdled over the seats, hot on his tail. She landed on the donkey's back, wrestling Marcus to the ground.

Students started whistling and hollering. "Shakespeare rocks!"

Ozzie walked to Emily, proudly looking at his ferret stone. "Things are going well, don't you think?"

❁ ❁ ❁

Lorren and Kara stepped out of the mirror and into a sticky mass of . . . something.

"Goldie?" Kara called, as she wiped at the silky strands covering her face.

"Icky!" The d'fly popped in front of Kara, pulling long, tacky strings off the blazing star.

"Are you okay?" Kara's heart pounded.

"Uh honk." Goldie flew up and fluttered happily onto Kara's shoulder.

Kara hugged her friend so tightly, the d'fly squeaked.

Then she looked around. She stood on a platform in a dark, narrow chamber. Dull lights emanated from yellowish crystals embedded in the walls. The high ceiling faded from view overhead, rising into darkness. Behind her was the mirror, a dull gray piece of glass ornately framed in carved metal. It stood on silver clawed feet. Everything was draped in shiny webbing.

"What is this stuff?" Kara asked, unsure if she really wanted to hear the answer.

"Phhhllaf!" Lorren spit out a mouthful. "Spiderwebs!" The boy appeared from the adjoining corridor.

"Eww!" Kara brushed at herself frantically, assisted by Goldie.

"Come on, let's get in and out of here as fast as possible."

She followed him through rusted metal doors that creaked with age.

Something skittered overhead in the darkness.

"Are you sure this place is empty?" Kara asked nervously.

"No," Lorren muttered, clearing a path with his sword to reveal a long corridor.

"Even if we find this rose, how do we find the stallion?"

"Don't know."

"How do you know where you're going?" Kara held Goldie close, eyes darting up, down, left, and right. She could hear the sound of tiny feet moving against stone. It seemed to be coming from everywhere at once.

"In here!" Lorren called.

She ran to catch up. In the gloomy dimness, Kara made out a large room of dark stone. Weak sunlight filtered in through tiny window slits in the sloping ceiling, illuminating thousands of twisting spiderwebs throughout the room. Cauldrons, dusty vials, cracking leather books, and mysterious metal structures were all draped by milky webs.

"It's the Spider Witch's lab," Lorren exclaimed, cautiously stepping deeper into the abandoned laboratory. "I heard she got really messed up using dark magic."

"What do you mean?" Kara asked, her breath quickening.

"She's like half fairy, half spider," Lorren continued. "Really creepy. Some wizard finally trapped the witch and her insect warrior and sent them to the Otherworlds. But that was way before I was even born."

Kara shuddered, thinking of twisted magic and dark dreams. "Let's just hurry."

"The flower won't be in plain sight." He pointed to the unicorn gem clutched in her hand. "Track it with your jewel."

Steeling herself, Kara edged forward, swiping webs aside with her hands. She held up her jewel, releasing a bright light.

A flash of pixilated insect eyes gleamed as a large bug buzzed into the light, dodging between the sticky webs.

"Gross!" Kara exclaimed, waving her jewel and bouncing light everywhere. "I hate bugs!"

"Probably just a few leftovers from the old tenants." Lorren noted.

Kara peered at a shelf strewn with broken glass and dried liquid. Signs hung below, written in strange slashes and markings. She squinted at the wavering writing. "What's this say?"

"Extremely dangerous spells. Don't look."

Kara jumped back involuntarily, then caught

herself. "Oh, that was so funny!" She edged around a wicked-looking machine with rusted metal spikes.

"I don't like this," Lorren said uneasily.

"This place could so use an interior decorator," Kara agreed, ducking under another web as she approached an iron table in the center of the room. "And a few tons of bleach."

"No, I mean, how did Tangoo know the elemental rose is here?" he asked, walking up to the opposite side of the cluttered table.

"Your secret club has inside information," Kara pointed out. "A powerful sorcerer like Tangoo must have ways of finding things out, too."

"He's a wily old goblin. I don't trust him," the prince stated.

"You keep saying that, but he's been trying to help me ever since I got here. He wants to help all of us!" Kara gingerly picked up an old book of spells.

"He works with quicksilver all the time to make the travel mirrors. He should know how to cure Lyra," the prince insisted. "I think Tangoo wants the crystal to do something else."

Exasperated, Kara slammed the rotting spellbook shut. "It seems to me if there's one person who really wants the power crystal, it's you!" she accused. "You found me first in the Queen's Forest, you were in the Fairy Ring, and when I let the fire stallion go, you took me to the rave to convince me to find it. It seems like you're willing to do anything to find that crystal!"

He looked at her steadily. "I believe Tangoo's plan could work. And I believe that if anyone could attract the crystal, it's you. You're the key to saving the Fairy Realms!" Lorren insisted. "You know me, I would never betray you."

"Know you?" Kara echoed, walking away from the table and casting a beam of unicorn light on another section of the room. "You and your Batman act? I have more reason to trust Tangoo than to trust you. He's not hiding behind—"

Kara broke off in mid-sentence. Her unicorn jewel had suddenly sparked bright white as she walked by an iron door. She winced, terrified that her jewel would explode with uncontrolled magic, but it held steady.

The boy rushed to her side. "Help me push this open."

They shoved the door inward and cautiously peered inside.

"Nothing here but plain stone," Lorren observed, walking into the empty room.

"No, look!" Kara pointed at a dark red mark on a block of stone near the floor. Kneeling down, she shuddered as a spiderweb brushed the back of her neck. Deeply carved into the stone was a small red spider. But what did it mean? On a hunch, she reached out and pushed the carving. Nothing happened.

"What now, Scooby Doo?" she muttered, standing up.

"Shh, wait!" Lorren leaned closer to the wall.

A faint noise, like a latch clicking, sounded deep inside the stone. Without warning, an entire section of wall sank soundlessly into the floor and vanished. Behind it was a huge chamber. Unlike the laboratory, there were no spiderwebs in the pristine space. The high walls were lined with ornately decorative tapestries.

Kara held up her jewel, scanning the room. Bright diamond light fell over an altar of gleaming black marble against the far wall. And floating above it were two delicate roses entwined at the stems. They were both dark as midnight and gleamed with pale blue light.

"The roses!" Kara breathed, her face haloed in white by her shining unicorn jewel.

The fragile flowers seemed made of crystal, but their deep blue petals were alive with swirling elemental magic. Like the fire stallion, the flowers were creations of pure natural energy, bound together in an exquisite form.

Gulping a shuddering breath, she anxiously walked toward the altar.

"Careful," Lorren warned in a hushed voice. "There might be traps!"

But nothing happened as she approached the black marble and stood inches away from the impossibly beautiful flowers. The unicorn jewel illuminated the magical roses like a spotlight.

"Which one?" Lorren worried. "They both look the same."

"The bud with the dud is a rose to the nose, no . . ." Kara muttered, trying to remember the rhyme Tasha had told her. "The rose with the nose—why didn't I write it down! Let's just take both and figure it out later."

"No, it's too dangerous."

Kara closed her eyes in concentration and willed herself to remember Tasha's rhyme. "The flower with power is a nose rose . . ."

"The flower power is blue, but only one dud can be true," the prince said.

"No, no," Kara exclaimed.

"Great, now you made me forget it!" Lorren fretted.

"Oh, like you even remembered it to begin with." She stood on tiptoes and leaned in close to the flowers, sniffing. The first smelled awful, like rotting eggs. Coughing, she took a deep breath and smelled the second. A beautiful aroma of roses and lilacs wafted from the sparkling petals.

Smiling confidently, she reached out for the

stinky flower. Her jewel flashed as her hand closed around the smooth stem.

"The bloom with the fume is the flower with the power!" she cried triumphantly, pulling the rose free. Then she looked around at the room. Something wasn't right.

Goldie's jeweled eyes looked everywhere.

The sudden noise of claws skittering against stone surrounded them.

"What is that?" Kara asked, holding her gem tighter.

"Let's get out of here before—" Lorren stopped, looking behind her, eyes dark with terror.

The massive stones around the room were sliding apart.

Clutching the crystal flower, Kara spun around—and screamed. A hideous mass of spiders surged from behind the wall, a voracious black wave that came straight toward her. She backed up, but more grotesque insects advanced behind her in a seething dark carpet. The ceiling shuddered and cracked, raining a swarm of writhing bugs.

"Eewwee!" Goldie swiped at the falling insects with her wings, batting them away from Kara.

"Ahhh!"

Thousands of black legs, putrid green abdomens, and oily wings glinted in the ghostly light as waves upon waves of gruesome bugs and spiders gushed from the walls.

Kara's gem exploded in light, spinning her back against the altar. She swung the jewel wildly, magic fire scorching an entire wall of bugs.

"Kara!" Lorren screamed.

The floor jolted beneath her, nearly sending her sprawling. The entire floor was sinking, drawing her down into a pit of squirming insects.

"Help!"

Suddenly, Lorren gripped her hand, pulling her onto the altar next to him. She scrambled up and stood watching as a sea of bugs rose below them. Centipedes, beetles, and spiders crawled out of the dank pit, clamoring for a foothold.

"I hate bugs!" Kara wildly swung the unicorn jewel, sending piles of bugs scattering.

Lorren slashed the top edge of the nearest tapestry, ripping an end free from the wall. "Hang on!"

He put his arm around Kara's waist and grabbed the loose end of the tapestry.

"Jump!"

Clinging to Lorren, Kara leaped as high as she could, and swung out over the teeming chamber. Shielding the rose with her curled body, she landed roughly on the stone floor and tumbled through the door.

"Run!" Lorren cried.

With Goldie hanging on, Kara scrambled to her feet and fled, yanking crawling beetles off her legs.

High-pitched shrieking scratched from thousands of tiny fanged mouths as the vicious swarm followed.

Running through the nearest cobweb-covered door, Kara and Lorren raced down the murky hallway and stopped short. The entrance to the mirror room was blocked with thousands of insects.

"How are we going to get to the mirror?!" Kara cried, panicked.

"We can't go back in there!" Lorren swerved to the right, leading Kara up a short flight of uneven stairs. She stumbled, but kept pace with Lorren, putting distance between them and the rustling black mass of slithering bugs.

Kara and Lorren dashed through a dilapidated set of huge doorways and skidded to a stop.

Before them lay an octagonal courtyard. At the far end an immense gleaming spiderweb stretched from the floor all the way to the highest turret.

Kara quickly made her way across the stone yard. Light reflected crazily off the silken strands, forming shadows as deep as a cave. Three shimmering black mirrors were imbedded in the sickly pearl-like threads. There were other things imbedded as well, large cocoons tightly wrapped, stuck to various points on the web. She didn't want to even think about whose snacks those were.

"Which mirror?" Kara cried, glancing nervously over her shoulder.

"I don't know!" Lorren exclaimed.

The bugs surged through the doors, hungry for their escaped prey.

"The rose!" Lorren exclaimed, reaching out for the shining crystal. "Give it to me!"

"What are you doing?" Kara whipped the precious elemental magic from his grasping hand.

"The spiders are protecting it. You'll be safe if I take it!"

Kara's stomach lurched. This was her only chance to save Lyra, and he was trying to take it from her. Then it hit her: He'd been using her all along, just like everyone else. All they wanted was her magic, her blazing star powers to save their world. Well, what about her world? Her world was Lyra!

"No one takes advantage of Kara Davies. You'll just have to find your own power crystal, Prince whoever you are." Kara jammed the rose into her pocket and ran toward the mirrors.

"Wait!" Lorren shouted desperately.

She pulled Mirabelle out and flipped the clamshell open.

"Princess." Mirabelle beamed. "How may I assist you in your radiance? Might I suggest some lip gloss—"

Kara held Mirabelle up, showing her the three gleaming mirrors. "Which one?"

"Well, the right one is nice, but it reflects several deep layers of astral planes."

"Then that one?" She swung the little mirror to the left.

"Excellent craftsmanship. But the shimmer seems off. Could be fatal to molecular reconstruction."

On the web above them, a dark shape shifted. Eight enormous hairy legs moved in horrifying syncopation as a gargantuan black spider rose from the web's center.

Goldie, Kara, and Mirabelle shrieked.

"Mirabelle! Which one?!"

"Ooo, I don't know, just jump!" the compact squealed.

Kara took one last glance at Lorren's horrified face and aimed herself toward the center mirror.

"See you on the other side, Prince Butthead."

She barreled into the center mirror.

"No, not that one!" Mirabelle screamed.

Kara plummeted through twisting, blinding space, clinging to Goldie. Dazzling lights streamed past her eyes spiraling to infinity. Suddenly she slowed, as if she were falling through water, then stopped. She found herself standing on an impossibly bright glowing plane of light.

Kara looked up at the tall, shimmering figure that stood before her.

"I've been waiting for you, blazing star," the Dark Sorceress said, smiling.

Chapter 11

"Stay away from me!" Kara yelled, recoiling from the Dark Sorceress. Had the mirror taken her to the Otherworlds?

"I'm not who you think I am," the tall woman said, her voice soft.

Kara shuddered, clutching her jewel protectively. Was this another trick? Suddenly Goldie flew to the woman's shoulder.

"No!" Kara cried.

"Hello, little one." The woman laughed. Silver hair draped her shoulders, falling over a shimmering dress. Goldie sat, calmly preening herself. "You are a very clever little dragon, aren't you?"

Goldie nodded.

The woman's warm eyes locked with Kara's.

Like the Dark Sorceress, she had deep green eyes and flowing silver hair. But the eyes were not cold reptilian slits, and her hair had no jagged lightning streaks. The Dark Sorceress's deeply etched features were set in cruel, mocking lines. This woman's face was soft and friendly. And fluttering behind, so delicate that Kara had not seen them before, were iridescent wings.

"Who are you?" Kara asked tremulously.

"I am Lucinda." Waves of radiant magic glowed around her as she moved closer.

"As in Queen Lucinda?" Kara asked, astonished.

"Yes," the woman smiled warmly.

"What is this place?" Kara looked around for the mirror that had brought her here, but a mist-like sparkling rain obscured visibility in every direction.

"You are inside the mirror, on the astral planes of fairy magic," Lucinda explained, her voice pure and sweet. Then her warm smile faded. "We must hurry—I can only shield you for a few minutes. They will sense you here."

"Who?"

"The Dark Sorceress and her allies."

"Is she really your sister?" Kara asked.

"We have grown apart."

"How can she be human, then?"

"The part of her that *was* human is long gone."

Kara stiffened, remembering the terrifying nightmares that reached for her. "They're trying to steal my magic."

"You are the blazing star," Lucinda said simply.

Kara hung her head.

Lucinda's bright eyes reflected the shimmering

of Kara's unicorn jewel. "The jewel that adorns your neck was once mine," she told the girl. "It has been waiting for the right match."

"You have the wrong girl."

"You are the spark, waiting to ignite a fire."

"Everyone is telling me what to do, but I don't even know who I am," Kara cried, feeling vulnerable and lost.

Lucinda's rosy lips curved in a gentle smile. All at once, glowing planes of light appeared, wavering and rippling, taking on dreamy, hazy images . . . scenes from Kara's memories. They began playing like movies before her eyes. She watched, transfixed.

Five years old—ignoring her mother's instructions, she swept from the beach into the ocean, terrified as the strong undertow pulled her down.

This is surreal, Kara thought, as the next one came.

Age eight—riding her favorite gelding, Sugarpie, in competition. The moment she had dreamed of, so sure she would come in first because she was always the best. She had come in third and had thrown a tantrum.

Age ten—Kara singing karaoke to Britney Spears and making a total spectacle of herself. Heather, Tiffany, and Molly were rolling and laughing so hard, they spit up their popcorn. She was always the most popular, always the center of attention.

Kara watched the memories continue to play

before her eyes. She was surprised that her emotions had grown stronger with time, how this videodiary shaped who she was and set the stage for what would come next.

Two girls she hadn't even known before, had nothing in common with, and who couldn't possibly know what she was all about. But they had something Kara didn't. Something beyond anything Kara had ever dreamed possible.

—Clumsy Emily walking a whole pack of dogs and getting herself completely entangled in the leashes. Tiffany and Heather were so mean to her, and Kara didn't do anything about it. . . . Kara was not proud of her first encounter with the healer.

—Dark-haired, tough Adriane, in Kara's face because Kara had promised not to tell anyone about the "purple bear," Phel, but that's exactly what she had done. Kara grimaced, knowing how she had jeopardized the lives of all the animals and the secret of Ravenswood.

—Kara placed her trembling hands on Emily's healing jewel and Adriane's wolf stone. Magic fire flooded through her senses. She didn't understand it, but knew she wanted it more than anything.

—Kara reached for the horn of the unicorn, stealing it from the Ravenswood Library. She didn't care what happened as long as she got the magic.

All Kara had wanted was her own jewel. How selfish that seemed now.

They had accepted her in spite of who she was:

spoiled, vain, and inconsiderate. But Kara had changed. She saw that now, as crystal clear as a mirror.

The images disappeared, and Lucinda stood before her. "What we leave behind makes us who we are."

"But what's wrong with me?" Kara cried. "Why can't I use my magic?"

"Because, Kara. The magic is not for you."

There it was. Panic twisted Kara's stomach. It had all been a mistake. The magic had never been meant for her.

"Kara, the gift of a blazing star is to make *others* shine more brightly. Not yourself."

Kara took a deep breath, trying to think it through. She had always been strongest with Adriane and Emily by her side, giving her magic to them.

"This is your time," Lucinda said softly. "You are a teenager, Kara, when the magic first comes alive. It is already being crafted, shaped like a fine sculpture. You can feel it, can't you?"

Kara nodded helplessly. Even now, she could feel the magic blazing inside of her. If she let it go, she feared she would blow apart, vanish like a dream.

"It's too strong," Kara cried. "I don't know how to use it."

"So many love you, and will help."

"Like Lyra." Kara lowered her eyes.

"Kara, there is something else."

Kara turned wide blue eyes to Lucinda.

"You have some idea of what the Dark Sorceress is capable of."

Kara nodded grimly.

"She covets your magic. Even though trapped, she reaches out through dreams." Lucinda's eyes flashed. "But make no mistake, she will strike again and she will strike hard."

Kara felt shivers down her back. "What could happen?" she whispered.

"Are you sure you want to see?"

Kara steeled herself. "Yes."

Lucinda waved her hand, summoning an unfamiliar set of images.

—A beautiful teenager, seventeen years old, golden blond hair trimmed neatly below her shoulders, stood at the entrance to the Ravenswood Preserve, cold blue eyes looking through a chain-link construction fence. Bulldozers cut through the still morning air, and trees toppled over as the destruction of the preserve began.

Shock, grief, and guilt consumed Kara. Why hadn't she stopped this from happening?

—The Dark Sorceress sat upon her throne, ready to command the vast armies at her feet. All she had to do was give the order, and worlds would be hers. The power of the magic was inescapable, growing, seducing, and infecting every part of her being.

Kara looked closer at the animal eyes of the sorceress and gasped. They were ice blue—Kara's eyes.

—Queen Kara lazily touched her unicorn jewel, then fingered two bracelets upon her wrist. Each held a different gem—the rainbow jewel and the wolf stone.

"That can't be what will happen!" Kara cried as the horrible images faded.

"That is up to you," Lucinda said.

"I won't use my magic!"

Kara would never risk all those terrible things.

"You cannot hide from your life just because there's a chance you might get hurt." Lucinda smiled gently. "The future is shaped by your choices. It is what makes you so powerful."

Kara nodded.

"You must chose to become the blazing star!" Lucinda's luminous form began to waver like a reflection in rippling water—

"Wait!" Kara cried

—But Kara was already moving, falling. She stepped out of the mirror blindly, wincing as bright light seared her eyes.

A sharp cry pierced the air—something was in agony.

Goldie was searching for the source.

"Where, Goldie?"

Goldie took off, Kara running behind.

They crested a grassy hill and skidded to a stop. Rocky outcroppings, brush, and tall reeds lined a river as it coiled like a snake through higher banks. In the distance, the mountains kept rising, blanketing the horizon with sparkling crystal peaks.

Another cry. Kara's heart twisted. Her jewel surged, compelling her to move forward. She ran, boots crunching through tough cattails.

Scrambling over jagged rocks, Kara followed the pull of her gem and rounded a bend. At the base of a rocky hill was a large hollow, protected by a jutting overhang. Goldie fluttered above, squeaking and screeching. The entire hollow glowed pale reddish orange, reflecting flames. The fire stallion flashed and fluttered, taking then losing shape.

Without thinking, Kara rushed forward, her heart pounding.

The stallion was down, entangled in wet grass and reeds. His fiery body sizzled and flickered as he lashed out with a flaming hoof, struggling to get to his feet. Redhot waves surged up, licking greedily at Goldie as if they would devour the small dragon.

"No!" Kara cried, dashing into the shallow waters. Desperation hit her like a fist. She could feel the horse's need pulling at her magic, drawing her closer.

The horse looked nothing like the awesome stallion she had seen less than a day ago in the arena. Spots on his flaming coat were dark, dissipating like dying coals.

Fire flared in swirls and loops, bursting into the

shape of a horse before melting back into pure flames. The horse was desperately trying to hold his form together.

"Please, let me help you," Kara implored. Sparks flew from her unicorn jewel as she stepped closer. She clamped down her magic and focused on the horse's ferocious need.

"Easy," she said. "I can help you."

The horse snorted smoke, fire streaking up and down his back, sending snaking tendrils into the sky. The spell that held him together was gone.

Kara moved closer, realizing that her unicorn jewel was protecting her from the intense heat. She reached into her jacket and pulled out the shining Blue Rose. The stallion's wide eyes locked on the swirling blue magic. Gasping, he struggled forward.

Kara felt her magic surge from her jewel, but she held it steady. Something had changed. Kara had reached another level of control.

The glimmering azure magic of the rose grew more intense. Closing her eyes in concentration, Kara reached out to the stallion. His wildly unstable magic trembled across her senses, pulling, grasping at her.

Magic fire burned through Kara, struggling for release. But she wasn't afraid. She opened her heart to the stallion—and let her magic go.

This time there was no crazy, unfocused explosion—just the Blue Rose blooming in her hand, its shimmering petals spreading and brightening. The rose slowly lost its form and changed into a ball of elemental magic. Spreading her hands, Kara washed the magic over the stallion.

Instantly a blast of heat surged from his body. Trails of raging fire pulled back and tightened into solid form. In one powerful movement, the stallion was on his feet, his strong muscles pulsing with whorls of brilliant fire. The reeds and swamp grass melted away in a hiss of smoke.

Stamping fiery hoofs, the huge stallion ran up the bank and stopped. He turned his golden eyes to Kara.

"Who are you?" the horse asked, bright flames trailing from his mane and tail.

"I'm Kara." She smiled.

The horse snorted, accepting her name.

"And you?"

The stallion reared, fire raging from his body. He stamped the ground, spilling flames across the damp grass.

Kara climbed up the bank and stood near the stallion. "What's wrong?"

"I have no name," the stallion cried, eyes flashing in pain and sadness.

Kara moved closer.

The stallion lowered his blazing orange head. She stretched out her hand wonderingly. As her fingers touched the stallion's glowing cheek, rays of brilliant magic flashed from her jewel, sending her long hair flowing back from her face and ruffling the stallion's fiery forelock. This was not the uncontrolled storm of magic fire she had come to fear. This was soft and gentle, full of love and kindness. The horse stepped back, but Kara moved forward, protected by her jewel, until her hand tamed the wild fire of his mane.

"You're so beautiful," she spoke softly, running her hand over his neck, settling the flames. "Like a star shining on my heart. I will call you Starfire."

The stallion stood straighter.

"Starfire. It is a good name," he said proudly.

The horse whinnied and snorted, prancing and dancing.

Kara laughed joyfully as Goldie tumbled happily above her head. The blazing star reached out impulsively and hugged the stallion's great neck. She felt the magic fire drumming through his form, a fierceness barely contained, as wild and intense as her own.

Starfire lowered his head over Kara's shoulder. She closed her eyes. They stood together on the bank listening to the river flowing gently past.

"What is it?" Kara pressed her face against Starfire's cheek, sensing his great need.

"I am fire," he said sadly, and Kara understood.

She saw the images from his mind. Tangoo had created the horse from Firemental magic, then locked him in a cage. Like the Blue Rose, the stallion was just a shell to hold magic; nothing more than a tool to be used to get the power crystal.

"We are both being used," Kara said.

"We will run away!" Starfire snorted.

"I can't do that. My friends need me."

"I don't understand." The stallion's voice was resigned.

Kara gazed at her new friend. He had been formed from fire. How could he choose anything when he had no one to help him, to love him?

"Do you remember anything else?" she asked.

The horse whinnied sadly. *"I have no past."*

Kara stepped back and stared into Starfire's brilliant golden eyes. "Then I'll give you mine."

Starfire returned her stare curiously.

Holding the unicorn jewel tightly, Kara closed her eyes and let the memories flood through her. Everything Lucinda had shown to her and more, she now gave to Starfire, freely, unconditionally, opening her heart and sharing the very essence of herself with the stallion. All the joy, pain, love, and loneliness of growing up. Images of her family, her friends, everything that meant something to her and, finally, Lyra.

The unicorn jewel streamed with dazzling light and entwined with the stallion's glowing red flames. Starfire's eyes opened in wonder.

Kara moved to his side. She grasped his mane

and leaped onto his back. Settling in, she felt as comfortable as if they had ridden together every day of their lives.

Suddenly Kara laughed aloud, stretching her arms wide, reveling in the strength of their combined magic. She had given Starfire a reason to live and the freedom to chose his own future. And, in return, he had freed her, too. Freed her to do what she must.

Sensing his bonded's need, Starfire reared. *"We must ride."*

Chapter 12

The rulers of the Five Kingdoms all sat in their respective thrones, waiting. The air bristled with energy, filling the ring with a sense of urgency that made the gathered crowds even more anxious.

Selinda rose and walked to the center of the ring. "I was hoping Tangoo's plan would work."

Queen Raelda joined her. "The blazing star was a worthy choice, but not even she can change the inevitable."

As if on cue, lightning split the skies overhead, leaving jagged streaks of purple and red.

"What say you, Tangoo?" Selinda spoke as the gaunt sorcerer approached. He looked haggard, as if he hadn't slept in weeks.

"We must have patience, my ladies." Tangoo's eyes darted up as another bolt tore a blaze of green through the sky.

"We are out of both patience and time," Raelda said brusquely, her face set in grim lines. "The Fairy Realms must be completely sealed off."

The Fairy Queen's intense violet eyes met Raelda's. "You know we cannot allow that. The web as we know it would be destroyed."

Raelda's gaze hardened. "So be it."

"Surely there must be another way," Selinda implored the Goblin Queen and her sorcerer.

Tangoo looked at the Fairy Queen. "Only Avalon's magic can save us."

Selinda raised her hand, drawing all eyes toward her. She took a deep breath and called out: "Before the die is cast and war is upon us, I ask our brothers and sisters of the Five Kingdoms: Is there anyone here who will ride for the fairies?"

Her challenge echoed over the Fairy Ring. It was met with silence.

Selinda took a breath and called out again. "Who will ride for the fairies?"

Suddenly, a thunderous roar shook the ground as a jagged bolt of lightning shot across the Fairy Ring. The crowd shrieked as fire blazed where the bolt had struck.

Then the firelight dimmed, and an awed silence washed over the crowds.

Kara sat proudly upon the fire stallion's back. The blazing star called out, her voice strong and confident, "We will ride for the fairies!"

Pandemonium broke out as the kings and queens all rose at once. Selinda, Raelda, and Tangoo rushed to the stallion's side.

"You see, I told you!" Tangoo's eyes were dancing with delight.

"Well done, Princess Kara," Selinda said, smiling radiantly.

As Tangoo drew closer, the stallion stamped and snorted, his fire leaping and licking the air. Kara ran her hand over the mighty horse's neck, instantly calming the flames.

Raelda's eyes were wide in amazement. "Indeed, Princess. You have shown tremendous resolve."

"Yes, yes." Tangoo rubbed his hands together anxiously. "That is precisely why this plan will work."

"What do you require of us?" Kara asked.

Tangoo rushed to the mirror by Selinda's throne, his long, patterned robes billowing out behind him.

"The princess and the fire stallion will jump through a series of four mirrors," he explained. "Each mirror leads to a place of extremely strong elemental magic. You must gather enough magic to forge four talismans, one each of water, air, earth, and fire."

"So the magic will take form like the Blue Rose," Kara said. She felt Starfire tense.

"Precisely, Princess." Tangoo pulled a shimmering silver pack from beside the mirror and handed it to her. "Place the talismans in here. The combination of the four should be enough to attract the power crystal."

Kara nodded, slinging the pack over her shoulders.

"A fifth mirror will return you here, to the Fairy Ring." Tangoo's black eyes seemed to bore into her. "I have every confidence that events will unfold *exactly* as I have planned."

Over the chatter of the excited crowd, Raelda said, "I am sure I speak for everyone here, Princess Kara, when I wish you success. May your magic keep you safe."

"Thank you." Kara nodded her head respectfully, then scanned the ring for Lorren. But the boy wasn't there. She felt a sudden pang of guilt. She hoped he had made it safely back from the Spider Witch's lair. At least there was one thing she knew for sure. She patted the fire stallion, this creature forged from magic, now risking his life for her. The blazing star and the Firemental stallion, their destinies intertwined, riding for Lyra, for the Fairy Realms, the magic web, and Avalon itself.

Kara looked to Goldie and smiled gratefully. Without Goldie, Kara would never have made it this far.

Kara thought of Lyra and everyone else depending on her. She would not let her friends down. It was time to become the blazing star.

Starfire reared, sending licks of fire streaking into the air. Kara held up her jewel, surrounding them with diamond-white magic. "We are ready," she called out.

The crowd surged to its feet, their cheers ringing into the skies.

Starfire leaped through the first mirror. Kara's long hair streamed behind her as they vanished into the rippling glass. The ride of the blazing star had begun.

❁ ❁ ❁

Kara and Starfire landed hard, the horse's fiery hooves melting tracks across a wide, icy ledge. They were in the foothills of a glistening mountain range. Before them a mammoth mountain of glittering ice towered into the sky.

"Ice mountains of the Troll Kingdom," Starfire snorted nervously as his molten hooves melted through the ledge supporting him. Plumes of steam rose from the ground as they started to sink.

"We'll have to move fast," Kara said, realizing the mountains were made entirely of ice.

"Kaaraa," Goldie squeaked, and pointed.

Kara looked up to the remote peak of the mountain. A bright spark winked in the sun.

"The mirror!" Kara cried. She held up her jewel, flashing beams of light into the sky. "Everyone ready?" she asked, leaning forward, letting the stallion's fiery mane envelop her.

"Ready!" Starfire stamped his hooves, eager to run.

"Let's ride!" Kara shouted

"Yippee!" Goldie squealed as Starfire shot like a bolt.

The stallion galloped to the base of the mountain, his heat leaving watery trails in the ice.

Kara focused on her magic, and on Lyra. Starfire's immense power blazed into her, steadying her, filling her with a new confidence she had never felt before. Streams of diamond sparkles burst from her jewel, trailing behind like a comet. Firemental stallion, blazing star, and dragonfly streaked up the mountain.

With a mighty leap, the stallion hurled into the air. They landed on a small outcropping about halfway up.

Starfire stamped his legs, the melting ice sizzling at his hooves. This only made him sink deeper.

"Water fights fire," Starfire said worriedly.

"Let's see if I can make you some leggings." Kara swung her unicorn jewel, sending the bright magic flowing over the horse's legs, protecting him from the corrosive ice. Starfire now shone fire red with bright diamond legs.

"Pretty," Goldie said.

"Thank you." Starfire admired his new look.

"No, there," the dragonfly pointed.

Crystalline sparkles mixed with the diamond magic whirling in the air before them, glowing pale blue.

"Elemental water magic," Starfire said.

"All righty, then." Kara fired a blast from her unicorn jewel, encasing the whirls, molding them into a mass of shiny blue light. "One talisman, hold the pickles," Kara said, thrilled with the new control over her magic.

She focused as the shards caved in on themselves, forming two lumps, elongating and stretching into—

"Oooo, bunny shoes!" Goldie pointed at the newly formed, long-eared purple shoes.

The shoes shuddered and fell to the ground. Ears flapping, they took off, running up the mountain face and disappearing out of sight.

"Lets hop to it!" Kara yelled, whipping her magic around them. Starfire bounded up the mountain, jumping from ledge to ledge, narrowly avoiding the cascading ice that rained down the frozen mountain.

"Hey, remember the time I threw my bunny slippers in the pool?" Kara laughed.

"I thought they were quite comfortable," Starfire said, focusing on Kara's memory.

Finally there were no more ledges in sight for Starfire to jump on to. Only the hissing river of the melting mountain, an avalanche of jagged ice floes rushing by.

Starfire turned in circles, snorting.

This was her first challenge. She was not about to fail. There had to be another way to get to the top of the mountain.

Looking at the melting ice, Kara suddenly

smiled. "When life gives you an iceberg, make some ice cream."

Kara pointed at the sheer mountain face behind them. Understanding her perfectly, Starfire wheeled around and faced the solid ice wall. Focusing their combined powers, Kara sent red, white, and Goldie magic boring into the mountainside. Kara bent low as the stallion dove into the mountain, melting a tunnel through the solid ice.

They punched through the other side, higher up than they'd been before. In a blur of movement, the purple bunny shoes scampered by on a thin, frosty path that coiled up the pointed pinnacle of the mountaintop. Starfire charged after them, careening around the path as it wound tighter and tighter.

"Now this is real power shopping," Kara yelled.

With all her strength and concentration, she scooped up the fleeing shoes with her magic. Goldie held open the silver bag as Kara tossed them inside.

"And I thought it was hard to find shoes at Neiman's."

Starfire rocketed around the last curve. The magic mirror was set into the mountain's peak.

Encouraged by her awesome new abilities, she grabbed Goldie and hugged Starfire's neck. "Let's see what's behind door number two." Kara held on tight as Starfire dove through the glistening mirror—

—pHOnk!

A strange honking noise reverberated as Kara and Starfire landed.

Starfire stood on a fluffy cloud floating high above a dense, leafy forest. Kara's stomach lurched as she looked down at the trees far below. Clinging to Starfire's neck, she closed her eyes, convinced they would sink through the billowing clouds.

"Air supports fire," the stallion reassured her. *"We will not fall."*

Kara looked around. What were they supposed to do here? A gust of wind moved them gently drifting between a collection of other puffy white clouds.

"There's nowhere else to go but another cloud," Kara mused, twirling her jewel in her fingers.

"We must leap!" Starfire bunched his fiery muscles and leaped onto the nearest cloud.

GONG!

As he landed, a deep ringing filled the air. "Hey! Musical clouds!" Kara looked at the other clouds, all of different sizes. "Jump to the next one."

The stallion soared over empty sky and onto a smaller cloud.

A high-pitched note chimed through the air, harmonizing with the other clouds.

Something about those three notes sounded familiar to Kara, part of a melody she couldn't quite place. . . .

"Try the others."

Starfire leaped to each of the clouds, until they had heard eight different musical notes.

What would Adriane and Emily do? They were good with music.

"I know. Maybe we can arrange them together!"

Starfire's coat blazed as he sent his elemental magic into the winds around them, summoning air. The clouds moved closer, puffing squeaks, gongs, dings, and rings.

"Okay, we'll have to hit the different clouds at the same time to make the song sound right," Kara fretted. "Starfire can do it. Goldie can play, too, but I'll fall right through."

"Your new shoes are made of water magic," Starfire pointed out.

"Clouds and water work together!" Kara exclaimed. "Huddle."

Goldie flew close to Kara's face as she leaned over Starfire's neck. "Feel the music. I'll tell you the right order, and jump when I say so!"

Goldie carefully opened the silver bag. The purple shoes hopped into Kara's hands. She slid off Starfire's back, closing her eyes as she slipped into the bunny shoes and touched the cloud. Taking a deep breath, she let go of the stallion—and stood atop the cloud.

"At least I don't have to sing," Kara muttered.

Goldie flew about the clouds excitedly.

"Okay Starfire, you first!" Kara raised her arms, pointing to a puffy cloud.

Starfire jumped and landed with a powerful *Bong*!

"Goldie, now you," she said, pointing to the small cloud.

Goldie bounced up and down, releasing a flurry of notes.

Kara jumped, adding her musical harmony.

Conducting the cloud symphony, Kara sang along as she, Starfire, and Goldie created the chorus of her favorite Be*Tween song.

"I'm—on a—su-per-nat-ural—high!"

As the last note filled the air, the clouds swirled with glittering white magic. Starfire was on Kara's cloud in an instant, and she scrambled onto his back. The clouds continued to swirl in on themselves, gathering together to form an elemental air talisman. It was a pearly U-shaped frame, with eight golden strings.

"A harp." Kara smiled.

"No bunnies?" Goldie frowned.

A lone cloud drifted nearby, a shimmering mirror shinning in its center.

"Go!" she ordered.

A ripple of light flashed through the stallion as his fire sprang wildly out of shape. Kara felt it; for a split second he had lost his magic. Starfire leaped as Kara snatched the talisman in midair. She had completed two challenges, but Kara knew something was terribly wrong.

Chapter 13

Overwhelming darkness swallowed Kara, Starfire, and Goldie as they tumbled, free-falling out of the mirror until they finally landed.

Kara eased herself down from Starfire and gripped the horse's fiery flank to steady herself from pitching forward. The floor tilted steeply, making a screeching sound like rusted metal. "Where are we?" she asked,

"Dwarf mines," Starfire said, tottering precariously backward as Kara peered over the edge.

They had landed in some sort of mining car. Beneath the car, jewel light bounced off steel tracks that dropped into complete blackness. Kara gingerly took a half-step forward, and confirmed her fear—they were precariously perched on the tip of a terrifying drop.

"Nobody move!" Kara ordered.

Everyone froze as the car teetered forward and back.

"Affg. . . ." Goldie slapped her feet to her mouth.

"Goldie!" Kara hissed.

"Ahhh. . . ." The d'fly's cheeks puffed out.

Kara put her finger under Goldie's nose and the mini relaxed.

"Whew." They all breathed a sigh of relief.

"AH-CHOOOIE!"

The car lurched forward and plunged straight down into the black, dropping like a runaway roller coaster.

"Ahh!"

"Ahhhhhhhh!"

"Neighhhhh!"

Kara's stomach rolled over as the car plummeted through blinding gloom. She clung to Starfire. Goldie clung to her neck.

The car swung wildly around a bend, then dropped again, whisking them farther down.

"Where's the breaks?" Kara screamed, grabbing the edge of the car, her knuckles white.

The car veered up and around sharp corners, swinging Kara and crew back and forth, finally lurching to a sudden stop at the cavern floor.

"Watch that first step." Kara staggered to her feet and clambered out.

Starfire leaped out and sniffed the air.

The trio gazed in awe at an immense underground grotto. Pools of silvery liquid cast steely shadows upon the high walls soaring above them.

Some pools lay still, but sudden violent currents churned others, swirling the smooth surfaces.

"Quicksilver," Starfire warned. *"It's very volatile."*

"Quicksilver?" Kara flashed on Lyra, melting in the goblin laboratory. Looking at her own distorted reflection in a silver pool, her throat ached.

The quicksilver sizzled and popped, exploding in a frothing mass of bubbling liquid. Kara backed away and ran her hands over Starfire's flaming hide. She could sense the horse's fatigue. "How are you doing?"

"I am still here," the horse snorted.

Kara glanced at the silver pack, glowing on her back. "We have two talismans. Let's use one to increase your magic."

"No," Starfire said sternly. *"We need them to attract the power crystal."*

Kara bit her lip. She steeled herself and surveyed the area. "Where to?"

Goldie sprang into the air, pointing like a little retriever.

On the far side of the cavern, a corridor disappeared into darkness.

"Let's go," the stallion said. Kara was already swinging up onto his back.

Starfire carefully threaded his way through the bubbling quicksilver and trotted into the dark corridor. Feeling her jewel pulse, Kara slowly released a tendril of magic, watching it snake forth.

"I can feel it pulling at my magic!" Kara's voice echoed down the dark passage. Starfire snorted anxiously. *"There is strong elemental earth magic ahead."*

The unicorn gem illuminated shimmering walls leading deep into the mines. Rounding a bend, the corridor split in two directions.

"It's a giant maze!" Kara realized.

The wall behind them trembled. With a roar like thunder, a section of it detached and shot toward them.

"Look out!" Kara screamed.

Starfire jumped just before the slab of rock slammed against the opposite side. Doubling back was no longer an option.

Suddenly a section of maze in front of them shuddered and disappeared as if the earth had swallowed it whole, opening up an entirely different section.

Goldie fluttered overhead, trying to survey the maze from above. But the little dragon was getting confused as walls opened and closed, hiding the correct direction to the maze's center.

Before they knew it, they had lost all sense of direction.

"This is worse than the time you couldn't find the pretzel kiosk at the galleria," Starfire said, picking up one of Kara's memories.

They stopped as one corridor forked out on either side of them.

There must be a way to navigate this moving maze, Kara thought. Her unicorn jewel could light up sections of the corridors, but they'd have to waste time exploring every dead end if they relied on light. Kara considered the other tools at hand. The bunny shoes wouldn't do much here, but what about the harp?

Reaching into the pack, Kara removed the instrument and plucked a few notes. The chorus of "Supernatural High" reverberated in the passage to her right, dramatically amplified. But the passage to her left seemed to swallow the music, leaving only a faint echoing.

"The passage to the right is a dead end," Kara announced. "The sound bounces right off a wall and makes it louder."

"But to the left is a long tunnel, making the music echo," Starfire concluded.

The stallion stepped into the left tunnel. A long passage stretched before them, and they advanced quickly until they came to another fork in the shifting maze. Kara strummed the harp. Following the echoes, they made swift progress, but the corridors were moving more rapidly as they traveled deeper into the mountain.

"We're getting close." Power snaked through Kara's senses, a tingling presence along her skin.

Rounding a curving wall, they found themselves suddenly standing at the edge of a giant quicksilver pool. Floating above it was a pulsing silver heart. The glistening heart turned slowly, reflecting twinkles of light around the dark walls.

"The Heart of the Mountain," Starfire said quietly. *"The heart is a strong vessel for distributing magic."*

Goldie flapped, pointing to the bright mirror on the other side. Behind them the sound of sliding stone closed in.

"Okay, Starfire, let's do it."

The stallion backed up a few steps, then took a running leap. Soaring over the pool, Kara reached out and grasped the gleaming heart as they plunged through the mirror—

—Crisp air lifted her hair and sent flames licking from Starfire. A dark and foreboding forest surrounded them, deep woods where the sunlight could not penetrate and all was cloaked in shadow.

A bolt of jagged lightning seared across the sky.

Kara's pack now contained three talismans of elemental magic, symbolizing water, air, and earth—which meant this new one had to be fire. But in a forest?

She felt a tremor run through Starfire as howls erupted from the forest.

"Something comes." Starfire shifted, ready to run.

Kara's jewel burned hot against her chest. Something itched along her arms, a darkness clawing at her, turning her stomach.

"We will outrun them." With his fiery legs still protected by Kara's diamond magic, the stallion took off at a gallop. Twigs and leaves flew as his hooves pounded the earth.

Kara bent low, intent on one thing: finding the fire talisman. Holding her jewel high, magic streamed behind them.

Everything was a mass of shadows and mist as the woodlands flew past. Kara leaned forward, Goldie clutched close. She watched the timber begin to thicken steadily around them as they charged through leaf-strewn gullies, leaping over deep hollows and log-jammed ravines.

Suddenly, Kara was jolted forward, nearly knocked off, as Starfire reared and spun. Flashes of black fur and snarling teeth were all Kara saw as the horse erupted in flames. Something huge had lunged into their path, sideswiping the stallion. The ridge-backed beast stood upright like a man, with a long, spiked tail keeping it balanced. Massive claws on long fingers flailed as it sprang forward on powerful legs. Kara's jewel blasted diamond light, throwing the beast back as Starfire charged forward.

Three more of the things leaped from behind trees, trying to bring down the stallion.

"Are you okay?" Kara cried, watching fire trail behind them in long tendrils.

"Yes, hang on," Starfire cried, dodging between two beasts.

Before them lay a twisting path of glowing purple trees arcing through the forest.

"They must be markers," Kara exclaimed. "Follow them!"

Starfire galloped onto a wide path laid out like a bright racecourse. As he passed each purple tree, their trunks and branches flashed and glimmered back to green, illuminating the whole forest with an eerie emerald glow.

They were far from safe—more and more creatures were joining the race, closing in from all sides. There were packs of scaly lizards and dozens of snarling wolf-like creatures, all charging after them.

Two lizards blocked the stallion's path, heedless of Starfire's flaming hide. But the stallion leaped high, trailing fire over their howling fury.

Starfire staggered as he hit the ground, stumbling, unable to stop Kara from pitching forward. She watched in horror as Starfire lost all form, erupting into pure flame, then sprang instantly back to his horse shape. Fear ripped through her. Starfire was fading fast.

"Hang on, Starfire!" she cried. She could feel his magic depleting as if it were her own. The spell that Tangoo had used to create him had an expiration date: It was never designed to last. Now, whatever magic he had left, he was giving to Kara in a last desperate race to save the Fairy Relams.

Starfire plunged through towering oaks and elms that surged from of the ground like massive spears. And still the creatures came after them.

Kara saw the line of purple trees end a short distance ahead, seeming to lead into a wide clearing. "We're almost there!" she shouted.

They shot through the last line of trees like a blazing comet, streaking full force onto the field.

Behind them they heard the rush of mighty winds as the forest gave up its magic. Brilliant orange-yellow flashes surged from the trees forming a whirling ball of elemental energy. It launched into the field, drawn to the fire stallion and rider. Kara pulled Starfire in a tight circle as the glittering energy formed a golden stone, sparkling with the magic of sun fire.

"There it is!" Kara cried, urging the horse forward. Reaching out with her hands, she sent her magic to ensnare the last talisman. The golden sunstone gushed light as she jammed it into the bag with the other talismans. The bag billowed, the elemental magic binding together in a storm of dazzling power. Streaming magic, the stallion raced forward.

"Where's the mirror?" Kara cried to Starfire and Goldie, wind whipping her hair into her eyes. She scanned the area. Deep woods lay to the right, left, and behind her. Ahead lay a vast, open plain with rolling hills. Then something sparkled over the next hill, reflecting sunlight. "There!"

Despite the intense power surrounding the trio, Starfire was slowing down. Fearfully, Kara glanced behind them. The pack of beasts had broken from the woods and was gaining on them.

"Starfire, take the magic!" she screamed, pushing the bag of talismans against his fiery hide. "Use it for yourself!"

The horse ignored her. Head lowered, he pushed faster, shimmering in and out of shape.

Kara felt it before she saw it. The air above her rented, splitting open with a jagged tear. An incredible glittering jewel of blues and greens skimmed behind her just out of reach, gliding on the air streams of elemental magic.

The power crystal! The talismans had done what they were supposed to: attracted the power crystal of Avalon.

Behind them, the horde of beasts closed in, howling and roaring, driven mad with the desire for magic.

Starfire raced up an incline and skidded to an abrupt stop, fire spilling across the damp ground.

Kara's heart sank.

It wasn't a mirror she had seen reflecting the light.

Before them stretched an immense lake with deep blue waters as smooth as glass.

No way could the horse leap over it. It would be death for the fire stallion to jump into it. Kara swung Starfire around, but it was too late.

The creatures were fanning out on all sides, surrounding them, edging closer and closer.

The power crystal bobbed gently, floating on the mass of elemental magic behind her. She desperately tried to pull the crystal to her, but every second that went by, she felt the stallion fading away and, with it, her own magic.

Suddenly she heard the *thwack-thwack* of flapping wings overhead. A giant bat dove into the charging beasts. Glittering sword flashing, the masked rider shouted and screamed, fighting the monsters and pushing them back.

"Lorren!"

Kara jumped off Starfire, hit the ground, and slipped, the world spinning dizzyingly around her. She was so weak. But she grabbed the silver pack of talismans and struggled forward, each step a Herculean effort. Screaming, Kara reached out, desperately trying to pull the power crystal toward her.

Suddenly, another bat and masked rider swooped from the skies. A second Forest Prince? What was going on here?

"Princess, throw it to me," the first boy yelled,

struggling to block the magic-starved beasts from advancing.

Goldie fluttered wildly about Kara's head, blocking the second masked rider's grasping hands.

She blinked in disbelief. One of them was the real Lorren. The other, an imposter. She hesitated, not knowing which Lorren to trust.

"Princess, I'm the real me!" the first boy yelled as the beasts pushed past him, advancing on Kara. "Can't you see what he's trying to do?"

Goldie shot in front of Kara protectively.

"Hey, look! Magic!" the first masked rider yelled to the creatures. Pulling out a small, clam-shaped object, he flipped it open.

"Princess! You're so pale," the object exclaimed. "Do you need some blush?"

It was Mirabelle! Kara searched her pockets frantically. She must have dropped the small compact when she escaped from the Spider Witch's lair.

Ahhh!" The mirror screamed shut as the horde of beasts turned and grabbed for the enchanted object. Lorren took off, the mass of creatures giving chase.

"Lorren!" That had to be Lorren. But then who was the other—

The second rider angled his bat and swatted Goldie away. With a black-gloved hand, he reached out and wrested the bag of elemental talismans from Kara. She was too weak to resist.

The power crystal swerved away from Kara and flew to the rider.

"What I'm *trying* to do is remove that pimply pimpernel of a prince from ever irritating me again," the masked rider cackled, but it was not Lorren's voice.

"Tangoo!" Kara exclaimed.

"Oh come now, don't act so surprised. You think I could stand one more day listening to that constant bickering? Fairies complaining, goblins fighting, trolls bellowing, elves whining, do this Tangoo, do that, Tangoo, save us, Tangoo, blah, blah, blah!" he groused. "I'm amazed I didn't turn myself into quicksilver!"

Fear tore through Kara as realization struck home.

The sorcerer's black eyes shone behind the dark mask. "The time has come for a new order in the Fairy Realms, and the construction of a new web. Avalon is finished. You made sure of that yourself when you released all the magic."

"Lyra, what about Lyra?" Kara sobbed.

"Ah, yes. I know how strong the bond is between mages and their animals. How could you resist getting the crystal for me?" He laughed. "My quicksilver spells work much too well. Say bye-bye to your wretched kitty."

It wasn't Kara's magic that hurt Lyra! This was all set up, carefully orchestrated by Tangoo. Now he was going to steal the power crystal and blame the whole thing on the Forest Prince. She had been wrong about Lorren from the start.

"Nice job collecting the magic, Princess, but I have a much better use for it." Tangoo held up the bag of talismans in one hand and turned the power crystal toward the lake. Light flashed from the crystal, spilling over the waters. The surface glimmered with intense blue, then rippled to gray as the entire lake transformed into solid quicksilver.

"The lake is the last mirror!" Kara realized.

"Kara," Starfire was on his knees, breathing hard, fire streaming from his form. He struggled to stay whole, but Kara felt his Firemental magic breaking away. There wasn't much time left until he dissolved into pure elemental energy.

"He needs the talismans!" Kara screamed to Tangoo.

"The Firemental has served his purpose beyond all my expectations," Tangoo said, smiling evilly. "In fact, so have you, Princess."

Kara felt the magic drain from her. She fell to the stallion's side, hugging him fiercely as if she could keep his life from slipping away.

"Please," Kara pleaded. "He needs the elemental magic!"

"And I just happen to have an extra-special talisman, just for him." Tangoo reached into his pocket and held up a sparkling dark blue flower.

"No!" Kara screamed, realizing what it was. The second Blue Rose.

But it was too late. Tangoo threw the deadly magic at the stallion. The talisman exploded into Starfire. Sparkling black energy raced over his body, eating away the last of the elemental spell.

Starfire's eyes locked with Kara.

"Remember me," he said. The horse erupted into a final ball of flame and vanished.

Kara was hurled backward. She tumbled down the incline, sliding out across the slippery surface of the lake mirror.

"Time to say bye-bye, Princess," the goblin sorcerer sneered.

Helpless and too weak to stop it, Kara's unicorn jewel exploded with the last of her power. She was enveloped in blazing light as a crackling beam shot from the lake and sizzled through the air. All of her magic was wrested from her, reflected into a blazing beacon reaching high in the sky.

The sky, already weakened by constant lighting, crackled and ripped, revealing a swirling mass of electric purple. Her breath caught in a silent scream. She was looking into the Otherworlds.

Kara felt the mirror drop away below her as she fell through—and landed with blinding lights shining in her face and the thunder of applause in her ears.

Kara blinked the light from her eyes, expecting to see fairies and elves and trolls in the Fairy Ring.

Instead, she saw her math teacher, her brother, and the entire student body of Stonehill Middle School on their feet, clapping.

The mirror had dropped her center stage, right in the middle of the school play.

Chapter 14

Kara stood frozen in shock, the last of her radiant magic drifting away like dying embers of a fire. Her jewel lay cold and lifeless against her heaving chest. Starfire was gone, and soon the Fairy Realms would follow. And Lyra. All because of her.?

Eyes stinging with tears, she looked offstage, desperately searching for Emily.

" 'I will sing!' Hee honk!" A tall boy was standing next to her, wearing an amazingly realistic donkey costume. Even his long hairy ears were twitching. " 'That they shall hear I am not afraid'."

She then remembered the play, *A Midsummer Night's Dream.* Marcus was reading the character of Nick Bottom, who gets turned into a donkey. He didn't even notice she had just crashed the play.

A tall girl with long blond hair wearing a bright pink fairy princess costume hung on the donkey's arm—was that Adriane?

" 'I pray thee gentle mortal, sing again,' "

Adriane read dramatically from the donkey's book. " 'Mine ear is much enamour'd of thy note.' "

Kara gasped at hearing her own voice coming from the warrior's mouth.

"Gah!"

Offstage, Ozzie was hopping up and down, waving his gleaming ferret stone. He was trying to contain Barney, Fred, Blaze, and Fiona inside Emily's backpack as they chattered with Goldie.

Thank goodness Goldie was okay.

Emily stood next to them, face scrunched in concentration, her rainbow jewel pulsing. But Kara couldn't hear what the healer was trying to say.

Finally Emily just blurted out, "Kara!? Can't you hear me?"

"It's gone!" Kara wailed. "It's all gone."

Tiffany, Heather, and Molly, their eyes twinkling under the spell of love, tackled Musso, sliding across the stage in a heap. Heather plopped French fries down the hobgoblin's mouth. "Here you go, my dashing, handsome, lovebug!"

"Splaff!" Fries flew out of Musso's mouth as the hobgoblin met Kara's gaze. "Princess!" He scrambled to his feet, looking everywhere. "There must be a portal here somewhere!"

The three fairies chased after him as Kyle suddenly sprinted across the stage.

" 'Be gone, thou fawning, dizzy-eyed giglet,' " he screamed.

Hot on his heels, Rae charged after him. "Come hither, thou cutiest patootiest!"

They plowed through the Fairy Ring, running circles around the actors.

Had the entire world gone nuts? Kara felt a nudging at her side. "Here," the donkey whispered, shoving a book into her hands and pointing to lines.

She stared at the book—it was the scene where her character, Queen Titania, falls in love with the Nick Bottom donkey.

"Wow—two Fairy Queens!" Someone in the audience exclaimed, as others cheered.

Startled, Kara blurted out her line, " 'What angel wakes me from my flow'ry bed—' " and burst into tears.

"She's good."

ZzzappPP!

A beam of golden wolf magic collided with Kara.

"Ahhh!" Kara staggered back.

The audience, riveted now, clapped at the innovative special effects.

Adriane grabbed the donkey, gem blazing. "Nobody sweet-talks my jackass!"

Someone wearing a papier-mâché wall costume suddenly ran onstage, pushed past the three leaping fairies and hopping hobgoblin, and stood between the two queens. A rainbow gem glowed from the wall's wrist, protruding from the costume's side.

"Emily!" Kara cried. "Everything's gone wrong! My magic is all gone, I lost Starfire, and Lyra's almost melted, the goblin sorcerer betrayed everyone, he's opening the Otherworlds, Lorren is being chased by monsters, the Fairy Realms are falling apart—"

"What page is that?" the donkey asked, scratching his head.

"I have to go back!" Kara exclaimed, holding up her jewel.

"Put down the jewel and step away from the donkey!" Adriane yelled, storming around the wall.

"What is with her?!" Kara asked.

"They're all under love spells." Emily explained. "Courtesy of the d'flies."

Kara gulped. So that was what Goldie had intercepted in Tangoo's lab!

Musso barged over. "Where's the portal?"

Heather, Tiffany, and Molly scrambled after the hobgoblin.

Adriane raised her glowing wolf stone.

Everyone onstage was crowding around Kara.

"I have to go back!" she cried. "Starfire!"

WHOOSH!

A fireball hurtled over the astonished audience and landed onstage.

The flames shimmered and took shape.

Kara's breath caught in her throat.

Strong and proud, the magnificent fire stallion stood before her.

"Starfire!" Kara flung her arms around his neck, sobbing in disbelief.

Magic surged through her, filling her jewel with fire and her heart with joy.

The stallion looked down, and Kara followed his gaze. Set into his powerful flaming chest was a gleaming power crystal, pulsing with magic.

"You got it!" Kara exclaimed.

"Our magic attracted a second crystal," the stallion explained.

"Two crystals!" She turned to Emily and gasped. "We got two crystals!"

"That is one amazing costume," the drama teacher approved. "It looks like it's really on fire!"

"It's those Ravenswood girls with their wild animals!" Kara's math teacher yelled disapprovingly.

"What kind of stunt is this?" the vice principal demanded.

Kara stammered.

Emily swept off the wall costume and smiled broadly to the audience. "We'd like to take this opportunity to announce the blazing-hot new tourist season at the Ravenswood Wildlife Preserve!" she cried out. "Everyone is invited to come on over and meet the animals! You won't believe your eyes!"

Emily took a bow as the audience cheered the impressive publicity stunt.

Kara leaped onto the stallion's back, her heart soaring as the magic rushed through her, fueled by the love of her bonded horse.

"Kara, give me a boost," Emily said. "Let's break these spells."

Aided by Starfire's strength, the blazing star reached out and grasped Emily's hand. Instead of flashy magic fire, Kara sent soft tendrils into Emily's jewel.

The healer smiled, impressed by Kara's elegant control. Her rainbow gem glowed bright blue, sending a spark of magic to the wolf stone on Adriane's wrist.

The warrior blinked and shook her head, staring incredulously at the fire stallion. "Kara? What's going on? Are you all right?"

"Yes!" she answered. And she was!

"Ewwww!" Heather shook her red hair and squealed, pulling herself away from Musso. "Where did you come from, Mars?!"

Molly and Tiffany took one look at the hobgoblin and ran offstage, screaming.

"Back to normal," Emily said, smiling.

Marcus shook his now human head as if he were waking from a dream. Scratchy donkey hair floated in the air around him. " 'And yet, to say the truth, reason and love keep little company together nowadays,' " he kept reading, oblivious of any change.

"I'm going back," Kara said to Emily and Adriane.

"We're coming with you!" Emily said adamantly.

"I'm the only one who can ride Starfire," Kara said. "But I won't be going alone."

Goldie popped onto Starfire's neck, in front of Kara, little fist raised.

"Let's ride!" she squeaked.

The horse kicked up onto his rear legs with a dramatic flare and charged up the center aisle, rocketing past the hooting and clapping students and out the main double doors. The standing ovation reverberated throughout the auditorium as cooling trails of flames vanished into thin air.

❁ ❁ ❁

Fueled by the pure magic of Avalon, the Firemental stallion returned to the Fairy Realms. Landing on the shore of the mirror lake, Kara, Goldie, and Starfire instantly felt the change, as if the air itself had mutated. The sky above flashed and whirled in seething coils of purple and glowing green. A fairy quake tore through the forests, twisting trees into dark and horrible shapes. The Fairy Realms were unraveling, for the darkness of the Otherworlds had already spread into the lake mirror, seeping into the lands.

Tangoo stood in the center of the mirror, the original power crystal in his raised hands, amplifying the towering beam of magic between the mirror and the Otherworlds.

"Princess!"

Kara turned to see Lorren running toward her, breathing hard.

"Lorren!" she shouted, relieved.

"Tangoo betrayed us all."

"I know," she hesitated.

"Listen to me," he said, looking into her eyes. "Tangoo is spreading the magic of the Otherworlds through the network of mirrors he set up."

Kara flashed on all the mirrors she had seen since arriving here. They had been placed in the most magical parts of the Five Kingdoms. No wonder the realms were falling apart so fast.

"You have to reverse the power!" he implored.

"I . . . how?" Even with Starfire, the power crystal, and her unicorn jewel, the task seemed immense, beyond her abilities.

"You are the blazing star, Kara," he said. "You are connected to the magic of Avalon itself."

"Oh, for crying out loud!" Tangoo's voice fell over them. "Give it up already, Princess. I'm sure my mistresses will be merciful if you join us."

"Stay away, Tangoo," Lorren cried. "You've done enough."

"Oh, but my plan is just beginning." He searched the forests for the hordes of creatures.

"Looking for your crew?" Lorren flashed a grin.

"Where are they?" Tangoo bellowed.

"They ran into a some "fairy" bad trouble." The boy let out a whistle.

Dozens of armed creatures emerged from the woods and ran forward to join the Forest Prince. Elfan, Spinnel, and Cotax were in the lead.

Kara recognized the creatures from the rave. They were Lorren's friends.

Tangoo focused on Kara, his black eyes glinting with rage. "No matter, Princess, the Otherworlds will replace the Fairy Realms," the sorcerer snarled. As if in response, the skies ripped open, sending beams of purple into the lake mirror.

Kara steeled herself, Starfire strong beside her, Goldie on her shoulder. Closing her eyes, she focused her unicorn jewel into Starfire's power crystal. Red-gold magic flared from his chest. She directed it toward the lake, trying to disrupt Tangoo's connection to the Otherworlds.

But Tangoo was not about to be foiled. He sent her magic slamming back at them. Flames skyrocketed from the stallion. Kara stumbled, reeling from the force of his attack.

"Twinkle twinkle, blazing star . . . how I wonder when you'll *die*!" the sorcerer snickered.

A jagged firebolt screamed across the sky and plunged into the forest. Foul plumes of purples and greens billowed in the distance.

"You can feel it, can't you?" he cried, eyes feverishly raised to the sky. "Dark magic seeps into the very core of the Fairy Realms, spreading like wildfire. Nothing can stop this, not even the blazing star."

The combination of the talismans, a power crystal, and the magic of the Otherworlds made Tangoo's power immense.

The earth rumbled beneath Kara's feet as waves of spiraling light surged from the mirror lake, forcing dark magic into the lands. She could feel the very fabric of the Fairy Realms ripping apart.

Lorren braced her, his hands on her shoulders. "Don't be afraid to be who you are," he said, his green eyes locked to hers. "Use your magic, Kara."

Her magic. The magic of the blazing star. Lucinda had told her the magic was strongest when it was used to help, to make others shine brightly.

"I can't do this alone." Kara's stomach twisted with panic. She needed her friends. But her jewel couldn't reach Emily and Adriane across worlds.

"I help!" Goldie flapped to Kara's shoulder, determination gleaming in her jeweled eyes.

"Goldie!" Kara exclaimed, remembering that the mini had bounced a love spell to the other d'flies. But she needed a lot more magic than a love spell.

"Can you connect me to Adriane and Emily's magic?"

Goldie leaped into the air, face scrunched in concentration.

Kara held on to Starfire's mane as another fairy quake warped through the forest behind them.

Then Goldie flashed, her wings shimmering, strong and vibrant, eyes glowing radiantly. "Let's rock!"

Kara held up her jewel and drew diamond light as Starfire flamed red fire. She wove their magic into a brilliant band and sent it shooting into the dragonfly.

"HooWeee!" The d'fly was engulfed in a flash of magic and blinked out.

Kara bit her lip, carefully adjusting the magical flow. Goldic had never transferred so much power before. Was her little friend up to it?

At first she didn't think anything was happening.

In her mind, Kara suddenly saw four bright flashes of magic. Goldie was linking with Fred, Fiona, Barney, and Blaze. Kara embraced the magic of each dragonfly, joining them to her and Starfire, until she had a view of all four of them, wingtips touching, twirling in a circle.

"Go Kaaraa!" Their happy voices squeaked.

Kara practically shouted with joy as the dragonflies' magic mixed with Starfire's and Goldie's. She had the weird sense of being two places at once.

Her body was in the Fairy Realms on the lakeshore, but her mind was on Earth, where she could see the now empty stage of the school auditorium.

Kara suddenly felt another boost of magic, kind and loving. She reached for it, connecting to the familiar blue magic of Emily's healing stone. The red-haired girl stood in the center of the dragonfly ring, eyes closed, jewel pulsing.

"Kara," Emily said warmly.

A jolt of wolf fire shot through Kara, strong and determined. Kara grasped the magic of the wolf stone as Adriane joined the circle, hands clasped in Emily's.

"I was hoping for a warrior, not a Fairy Queen," Kara said to her costumed friend.

"You can put a wolf in pink clothing, but she's still a wolf," Adriane replied with a grin.

"I can't do this without you," Kara cried.

"We are with you," they responded.

But an important piece was still missing.

Strong, fuzzy magic suddenly filled the gap as Ozzie stepped into the ring. His ferret stone glowed with power as he gave his magic freely.

Reaching out, she took Ozzie's gift.

"We love you, Kara," the ferret simply said.

And she was flying, gliding on glowing streams of magic, threading her way to Ravenswood. She flew through the thick woods, rich with greens. Beside her ran a black mistwolf, strong and proud.

Dreamer looked into Kara's eyes. *"I will always run with you, blazing star!"*

Kara felt the mistwolf's magic join her growing network as she soared high into the sky. Over the open fields, she found Tweek, riding atop the beautiful snow-white owl, Ariel.

"We are with you," the little Earth Fairimental yelled.

"As are we!" Voices echoed into the skies.

Below, the animals from Ravenswood stood together in the field, their voices joined in support. She welcomed them all to the expanding network, their magic thrilling her senses, filling her with new strength. She wrapped the magic of her friends around her.

There was no stopping her now.

As if summoned by her thoughts, the glimmering Ravenswood portal spiraled open in the field below, beckoning her on.

Kara shot through the portal and reached out for Aldenmor. She soared over the wondrous lands, now strong and vibrant, healed by the magic of her friends.

The howl of the mistwolves filled her with joy as the wolfsong washed through her senses. The pack, hundreds strong, thundered over a hill, lending their fierce strength to Kara. Bolstered by their power, the blazing star flew faster over the magical world, soaring above the glittering blue oceans.

Merpeople and seadragons cheered as Kara wove them into her ever-growing tapestry of magic and life.

She swept over the the old desert lair of the Dark Sorceress, now covered over with brilliant gardens. A sandy-haired boy stood beside a huge red dragon, sending Kara their magic through a bright red dragon stone. She felt Adriane's golden magic surge with happiness at the sight of her two friends, Zach and the Drake.

Whirling figures of earth, air, and water converged.

"The magic is with you now and forever!" Gwigg, the Earth Fairimental, called out.

Kara gasped as the incredible power of the Fairimentals joined her web of friends. She reached to Starfire, his fire taming her, keeping her in control.

Blazing with light, Kara soared across the lands as the magic of Aldenmor itself—the trees, the mountains, every living thing, big and small—sent its magic to her.

Kara could barely contain the building forces as she flung herself across the glittering magic web. Careening along arcs of stars, she reached for the most powerful of magical animals. Dazzling flashes popped along the looping strands. Crystal horns in all colors of the rainbow flooded Kara with power as the unicorns' mighty hooves thundered across the web. Thirty smaller horns chorused in perfect harmony as the Unicorn Academy happily added their song.

The rush of power made Kara laugh aloud. It thrilled through every part of her being. Everyone was giving his or her unique magic to Kara, each link connecting to everything else.

She was ready!

Kara soared into the Fairy Realms and swept through the Fairy Ring. The kings and queens quickly gathered the crowds into the center of the ring. Clasping hands, they all joined together to aid the blazing star.

Kara sped through the Fairy Realms like lightning, releasing her network's vast well of magic through the mountains—forests—lakes—rivers—into the very fabric of the land.

She vaguely sensed her physical body enveloped in a tempest of power. Something was tugging insistently at her mind. She suddenly realized Emily and Adriane were trying desperately to pull her back.

There was too much magic flooding through her. She was blazing out of control, too fast. Even Starfire could not pull her back now.

"Everyone uses the blazing star."

Through the dazzling brilliance, a presence was worming its way into Kara's mind, calling to her, drawing her in. Desperate, she grabbed for it and felt another magic, dark and compelling.

Anger welled inside Kara. Everyone was after

her power, using her for their own ends. The kings and queens were no different from the packs of magic-starved creatures, or even Lorren. None of them cared what happened to her as long as her magic was theirs to use.

"The magic is yours. It is time for you *to use it!"*

The magical network flickered, its brilliant light taking on darker hues. Kara felt the magic of the Otherworlds working through her, infecting each level of her network.

The white-hot center of her magic blazed as the seductive force engulfed her. She felt the need and thirst and hunger for more magic. It would never be enough. She could twist the magic of all those linked to her however she wanted, reweave worlds any way her heart desired. And no one could stop her.

No! Kara screamed, reaching for someone to help her.

She felt herself drowning, spiraling into the darkness, burning out like a blazing sunset.

"Kara."

Lost among the seething patterns of magic, she wondered where that voice was coming from.

"Kara! Hang on to me." Someone was supporting her with calm, strong magic.

Kara had a fleeting image of orange-spotted fur, sparking emerald eyes.

With a jolt, Kara came back to herself, trembling.

"Lyra?" she whispered. She reached for her friend. Lyra had never left her. The cat was always there, looking out for her. Watching over her.

Kara reached for the silver Heart of the Mountain, easily wresting its power from Tangoo's grasp. She sent the full force of her network through the quicksilver heart and focused on Lyra. She felt her friend's magic blaze to life, warm and loving.

Holding tight to Lyra, Kara let her friend's love wash over her, spreading back down the network.

One by one, she gently let the network go, breaking the hold of the dark forces.

Kara opened her eyes and stared at the mirror lake.

Starfire and Goldie were right by her side. Lorren stood nearby, watching her carefully.

Suddenly the boy leaped in the air and whooped. "You did it!"

Kara looked around. The lands were stable. No fairy quakes, no jagged lightning in the skies above. She had saved the Fairy Realms. No, she realized. Her friends had saved it through her.

A scream turned her attention back to the lake. Tangoo stood on the mirror, shaking with fear.

Kara had reversed the flow of magic. The mirror was now sending strong magic from the Fairy Realms, closing the Otherworlds.

She faced Tangoo, her heart filled with rage.

Tangoo held the power crystal in his hand. "If

you join us, the power will be yours," he said, flustered. "You can rule as you were meant to!"

Kara's ice blue eyes burned into the sorcerer. "Don't put it in your Day Planner."

She held up her unicorn jewel and fired.

Brilliant magic seared through the air. Tangoo swung the crystal to deflect the blast as Kara's fury smashed into him. Kara was jolted as the pure magic of Avalon touched the very soul of her being. She tried to pull her own magic back, but it bored into the power crystal with the full wrath of the blazing star. The jewel splintered and cracked, shattering into dust.

Screaming, Tangoo was caught in the mirror's powerful beam and sent hurtling up through the rift and into the Otherworlds.

The sky swirled in on itself, whirling with purples and greens. Great winds screeched over the rippling quicksilver. With a final burst of light, the rift closed. The lake shimmered and transformed back to shining crystal waters.

Kara stared at the blue sky, frozen. She had destroyed a power crystal, a crucial part of Avalon's magic. At the final moment, she had lost control of her magic after all.

Lorren stared at her, open mouthed. "You had it! You could have taken the crystal."

Kara hung her head. He was right. Tangoo was

helpless. She could have easily taken the power crystal.

"You still have another."

"Starfire!" she cried as the stallion's form rippled and wavered.

With a jolt of panic, Kara realized the stallion had let go of the second power crystal.

"No, you don't have to do this!" she cried.

"It is my choice," Starfire said gently. *"Avalon's magic beckons to me, I belong there now. I am with you, blazing star, now and forever."*

In a flash of Firemental magic, Starfire's stallion form dissolved and vanished.

Kara looked down, feeling the power crystal heavy in her hands.

"What happened to Starfire?" Lorren asked.

"He's free," Kara murmured. Her heart ached, but she did not feel the unbearable loss that she had expected. The stallion was still with her, a warm spark in the heart of her magic. He would give her strength and temper her fire forever, whether he was physically by her side or not.

She looked at Lorren and deposited the crystal into his hands. "This is what you wanted, isn't it?"

"A second crystal!" Lorren looked at her, amazed. "How did you do it, Princess?"

"I didn't. My friends did," she told him.

From out of the golden glow of the setting sun,

shimmering wings glittered. A large leopard-like cat, lustrous spotted coat bright and healthy, emerald eyes twinkling, flew across the lake.

Kara ran to the shore, tears streaming down her face.

The cat landed next to her.

Flinging her arms around Lyra's neck, Kara cried happily. "You're okay!"

"I'm glad to see you are in one piece, too," Lyra purred. *"Your magic reversed the quicksilver spell in time."*

Kara drew back, looking at her friend. "You saved me." She shivered with the memory of the dark magic pulling her under.

"I am always with you."

Kara hugged the cat, burying her face in silky orange fur.

Lyra eyed the power crystal clutched in Lorren's hand. *"I hope I didn't miss much."*

Kara smiled, suddenly exhausted. "Just the usual."

"That bad?" the cat asked, alarmed.

Kara sniffled, then laughed as Goldie landed on Lyra's head. She grabbed the mini and hugged her friends. "Let's go home."

Chapter 15

"This will never do!" Raelda yelled, sharp green eyes flashing.

"It is the only way!" Selinda shouted back.

"I fear you are wrong!" Raelda matched her peer's obstinate tone.

The stout Goblin Queen and the tall Fairy Queen faced off, staring defiantly at each other, faces flushed with anger.

"Ladies, ladies." Kara swept into the room, alarmed. "Your guests are waiting!"

"Ah, Princess Kara." Selinda stood back, arms crossed. "Would you please tell my stubborn neighbor that *my* choice is correct—"

"Kara, my dear," Raelda broke in, hands on hips. "Tell the most gracious Fairy Queen what is best for *my* ballroom." She waved her hands, indicating the vast room in Castle Garthwyn, which was lined by huge, bare windows.

Kara studied the two rolls of fabric covering a long

table. Selinda had chosen a flowery yellow damask. Raelda's selection was a deep blue velvet brocade.

"Curtains are *totally* crucial in any decorating scheme," Kara said, tapping her fingers to her chin. She scrutinized the completely opposite fabric selections, and then took in the sun-drenched ballroom. Rich oak paneling covered the high walls, and tiles of deep muted gold, like falling leaves, spanned the wide floor. "What this room needs is color . . ."

Selinda nodded smugly.

"But also regal elegance."

Raelda nodded back at Selinda.

"How about this?" Kara selected a roll of beautiful lavender sateen, accented with streaks of royal blues and deep violets.

"Not bad," Raelda mused, holding up the fabric.

"Royal yet colorful," Selinda agreed.

The two queens smiled at each other.

Lorren hurried into the ballroom, buttoning his black jacket and slicking back his dark hair.

"Whoa, this time we're gonna have a real war!"

"King Rolok?" Raelda asked.

"Everyone." Lorren smiled at Kara. "They've all been arguing ever since they got here."

Raelda led Kara out to the ballroom's grand balcony overlooking the grotto. "Come, we must settle this matter of your mentor."

"We've been doing fine by ourselves," Kara said.

"Tsk, tsk!" Raelda wagged her finger. "My dear, it is simply not proper for young mages to not have a mentor."

"Your power surprised even me," Selinda said seriously.

"She did everything you asked of her," Lorren muttered. "And more."

Raelda whispered loudly to Kara. "I've introduced him to every Goblin girl in the kingdom."

Kara glanced at the queen.

"But I think he has eyes for someone special," Raelda winked.

"Mother!" Lorren's cheeks flushed green.

"Oh, hush!" She slipped Kara's arm into his as they walked down the wide staircase. "Now escort the princess to the party!"

If not for the hundreds of frolicking guests and lively music, Garthwyn Grotto would have seemed a sanctuary hidden deep within the heart of the forest. Sparkling waterfalls tumbled down huge quartz rocks, filling a series of stone pools with crystal blue waters. Lush ferns grew near the glittering mist of waterfalls, and giant redwoods ringed the grotto like silent sentinels.

Guests from the Five Kingdoms were chatting, eating, laughing, and swimming, enjoying the spectacular afternoon.

All eyes turned to the princess of magic and the

Goblin Prince as they descended the gleaming marble staircase that led into the grotto.

Kara felt like Cinderella at the ball.

Kara and Lorren strolled near the food stands that lined the grotto's edge. Amazing pastries, strange-looking pizzas with green cheese, and bowls of purple chips and flower-shaped chocolates sat on tables jam-packed with endless varieties of snacks. A thick, yet delicious-smelling steam billowed from one table. The bright banner draped high above the grill proclaimed: MUSSO AND SPARKY'S MAGICALLY TASTY CHEESE!

Kara coughed, waving away a cloud of smoke, and smiled at the two fairy creatures working furiously over the hot grill. "I see you're on to your next daring mission."

"We're out of the adventuring game," Musso declared, smearing a gob of barbecue sauce on his white apron. His aviator cap had been replaced with a tall, puffy chef's hat. "With the Fairy Realms at peace, everyone's gonna want to rave."

"And our barbecued cheese sticks are going to be the life of any party!" Sparky added, waving a skewer dripping with cheese in the air.

"Not bad," Lorren said, sampling a cheesy bit.

Kara searched the crowd. With the Ravenswood portal now opened, all her friends had been invited to the celebration. She found them standing near a glittering waterfall, and waved.

Kara had given Emily and Adriane a complete

tour of the Fairy Palace before the party, including the magic closet. Emily looked beautiful with her hair piled into a mass of flame red ringlets and wearing a sky blue sundress and heeled beige sandals. Her healing jewel glowed with bright rainbow sparkles. Adriane stood next to her, gleaming dark hair pulled back in a simple ponytail. A wraparound white silk shirt set off her sparkling black eyes, with stylish jeans and matching jacket completing the outfit. Her golden wolf stone shone proudly upon her black and turquoise band.

Kara herself had chosen cream-colored linen drawstring Capris with small flowers embroidered on the hems, a matching pink tank top, and strappy off-white sandals. Her hair fell down her back in a cascade of gentle golden curls.

Dreamer dashed onto the sprawling lawns beyond the grotto, playing with a group of excited young pixies. Goldie zoomed around with Fiona, Fred, Blaze, and Barney sampling the snacks.

Kara walked toward her friends, Lorren at her side. "Emily, Adriane, this is Prince Lorren."

Healer and warrior grinned at the cute goblin.

Lorren bowed deeply. "Never has there been a day when such lovely ladies have graced Castle Garthwyn. Your beauty outshines your jewels."

Emily mouthed to Kara, *He's adorable!*

Kara blushed, then elbowed Lorren playfully. "Watch it Prince, your Zorro is leaking."

"No more disguises for me—I've hung up my cape," Lorren said. "My Zorro days are over."

"Aw, and we were looking forward to seeing the dashing mystery guy in action." Adriane grinned.

"A friend taught me not to hide who I really am." He smiled at Kara. "I'll be able to do more good as the Goblin Prince than I ever could have as the Forest Prince."

"Honored guests, your attention, please." Queen Raelda's voice rose above the clamor, commanding everyone's attention. A beaming young Goblin girl in green velvet robes stood beside her.

Raelda continued, "With the recent departure of our sorcerer, it is my pleasure to present the new Goblin court sorceress, the lady Tasha!"

As the guests clapped, Tasha ran to the mages. "Do you believe this?" she asked, giggling.

"You deserve it," Lorren told his friend, giving her a hug.

"Congratulations," Kara said with a warm smile.

"Now we must settle the matter of our princess," Dwarf King Rolok called out. "She must have a proper mentor."

The Dwarf King stood among a group of trolls, goblins, elves, dwarves, and fairies. In the center, shampooed, fluffed, and wearing a bright Hawaiian shirt, was Ozzie, trying to balance a plate piled high with waffles.

"Princess," Troll King Ragnar said. "You have

shown us brilliant power by saving our lands. But frankly, we could have given the Fairimentals not one power crystal, but two! Power such as yours, as well as the others', can be corrupted."

A chill ran down Kara's spine.

"We insist the mages accept a mentor from the dwarves!" King Rolok demanded. "After all, we are the hardest-working race in the Fairy Realms."

"Oh, I suppose you think fairies are just cute little woodfolk who spend their lives prancing about in the moonlight?" Fairy King Oriel demanded. "Well, we don't. We work!"

Brownies, spriggens, and sirens floating in pool chairs and sipping tall glasses of lemonade waved.

"Princess Kara, who would you chose to be your mentor?" Troll Queen Grethal asked.

"Hey, what about me!" Ozzie demanded. "The Fairimentals sent me to find the mages in the first place!"

"Sir Ozymandias, with all due respect, you are not trained in the magic and natural sciences," Dwarf King Rolok said dismissively.

"GaK! These are teenage girls, they don't come with instructions!" Ozzie sputtered.

"The mages need a fairy mentor," the Fairy King continued. "There's conjuring, spells, and spellsinging, black magic, white magic, wizard magic, witches' brews, horrible curses—"

"And what about focusing the magic?" the

Goblin King joined in. "There's magic mirrors, crystal balls, power jewels, talismans—"

"Gentlemen, ladies," Raelda called out. "Please, this is a party, not a debate."

"Tell us, young mage," King Rolok commanded, "what do you know about magic?"

Everyone stopped arguing as a hush fell over the entire party. All eyes turned to Kara.

"I know what I feel." Kara's hand went to her heart. "I know magic always starts here. And here, with my friends." She nodded, indicating Emily, Adriane, Ozzie, Dreamer, Goldie, and Lyra.

The healer and the warrior stepped forward and handed Kara the silver pack she'd gotten back from Tangoo. Even though Kara's magic had made the elemental talismans, they had never belonged to her. She understood that true power was not in using the talismans for herself, but in recognizing where they would do the most good.

Confidently, she stepped forward to address the kings and queens.

"King Ragnar and Queen Grethal," she said, turning to the massive trolls. "This gift is for you, so you may always feel the magic of laughter."

She handed the perplexed Troll King the shining purple bunny shoes. He broke out in a wide, toothy grin as he held up the elemental water magic.

The crowd cheered.

"King Landiwren and Queen Elara, this is for

you." She handed the Elf Queen the glowing pearly air elemental harp. "So you may always have the magic of music to inspire you."

The Elf Queen held the harp high in her graceful hand, setting off another round of applause.

"King Rolok and Queen Praxia." Kara took the Heart of the Mountain from the bag. All eyes went wide, appreciating the beauty of the glowing quicksilver heart. "For you, so you may always know the magic of love and kindness."

The dwarves cheered.

"And for you, Queen Raelda and King Voraxx," she said as she smiled at the goblins and placed the sparkling yellow sunstone in the queen's green hand, "so your wisdom and grace may shine over us all."

Raelda took the gift and hugged Kara tightly. "Thank you, Princess."

Finally, Kara turned to the fairy rulers. "Queen Selinda and King Oriel, I have a gift for you, too." Kara took the final talisman out of the bag and handed it to the queen.

Selinda gasped at the dazzling fire-red rose, exquisitely constructed from pure elemental magic. Its glowing light sparkled brightly in her violet eyes. "Child, where did you get this?"

"I made it." Kara paused. "Well, Tasha and Goldie helped me. It contains each of the four elements, working together to make strong magic."

Kara and Selinda hugged warmly.

"I shall treasure this always."

The crowd cheered.

Queen Selinda addressed the royalty, and all the creatures gathered. "I think the princess has shown us that, in spite of our differences, we are unified by a common cause: our love for our lands and respect for all living things. Is that not true magic?"

The crowd cheered in agreement, whistling and applauding enthusiastically.

"But what about a mentor?" King Rolok pressed.

Selinda smiled at Kara, Emily, and Adriane, then answered. "We will give the mages full access to *all* of our resources. We shall pledge to help them however we can, together."

Selinda smiled and reached for a silver carrying case. "Now, I have something for you, Princess." The case shook and rattled persistently. "They insisted."

The case popped open, releasing clouds of powder and perfume.

"We were born to beautify!" Skirmish cried joyfully, hugging Whiffle and squeezing another cloud of perfume from the atomizer's nose.

Puffdoggie leaped out, wriggling and barking, running circles around Kara's feet.

Mirabelle snapped open and closed excitedly. "We cannot bear to be parted from you again, Princess!"

"I will fluff! I will spritz!" Whiffle cried.

"Will you calm down!" Angelo yelled, pushing everyone in line.

Kara lit up—now it was her turn to cheer.

Emily and Adriane eyed the amazing accessories curiously, looked at each other, and shrugged.

Lorren walked to Kara. "You truly know how to work a crowd."

"I'm really a party mage." Kara giggled, then said seriously, "Lorren, I want you to know I didn't mean to destroy that other power crystal." She turned away. "At the last minute, I just lost it."

"After what Tangoo did, who could blame you? No one here, certainly." He looked into her eyes. "Kara, you never intended to destroy the crystal. It was an accident."

Kara wasn't convinced.

"You saved the Fairy Realms." Lorren clasped his hands over hers. "And together we'll find a way to save Avalon!"

"Okay." She smiled.

He bowed. "Now my friends are all insisting on dancing with the mages. So please help me or I may have to fight them off."

"Wait right here," she told Lorren, then dashed over to her friends.

Taking in the scene, Adriane quipped, "How are they ever going to keep Cinderella down on the farm?"

"That's your job," Kara responded, throwing her arms around Emily and Adriane's shoulders. "Whatever happens, I'm counting on all of you and . . ."

They looked at Kara.

"I love you all very much."

Lyra, Dreamer, Ozzie, Emily, Adriane, and Kara stood together, Goldie whirling overhead. Clasping hands to paws, the mages and their magical animal friends smiled at one another.

"Now let's dance!" Kara commanded.

Cotax spun Adriane on the dance floor as Emily whipped Ozzie into a ferret-stomping frenzy. Lorren and Tasha moved and shimmied, laughing as all the guests whirled around the floor in celebration, their joyous laughter filling the air.

Kara looked on and smiled. She raised her unicorn jewel and gazed into its light. Diamond white and red fire entwined and sparkled. Her magic had changed, and she with it. Starfire's magic had mixed with her own, strengthening and tempering her power. She was no longer trapped by her magic. She didn't fear it. Come what may, she was now free to choose *how* she would use it. She might make mistakes—correction, she probably would make mistakes—but there was no going back. The past shaped who she was. But the kind of person she would grow to be, well, that was all in her hands, like the magic running through her jewel. Her friends loved her. She knew that as sure as the bright sun shining over the wondrous Fairy Realms. But it wasn't about how much love she could gather in her life; it was how much she was willing to give back. That was the magic of the blazing star.

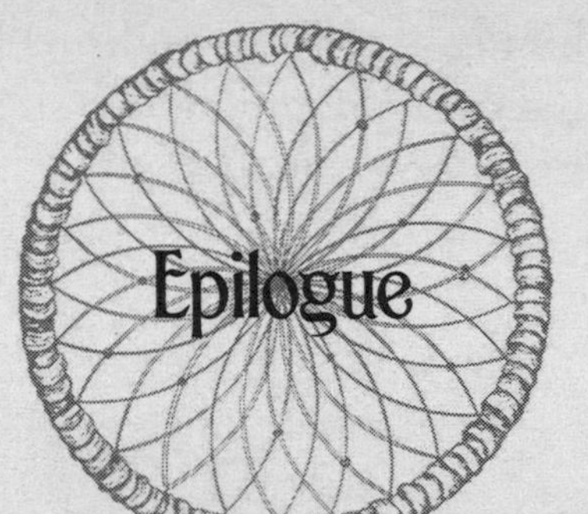

Epilogue

The gigantic black spider thrummed down its web, dragging cocooned bodies past the three black mirrors embedded in the silken strands. Long, spiked legs paused as it hissed at a cloaked figure that stood below.

"Yes, my pet, I missed you, too." The Spider Witch laughed, pixilated eyes roving gleefully around the octagonal courtyard of her lair.

The Dark Sorceress stood a few steps back, watching uneasily as her ally stroked the spider's massive head.

Appendages wriggling, the spider's huge fangs slipped from its mouth, sinking into a carcass as it began to feed.

The Dark Sorceress turned away, shuddering as the spider clicked and slurped. There were some things not even she could stomach.

The witch's insect warrior, standing across the courtyard, smiled wickedly at the sorceress's disgust.

The Dark Sorceress cursed herself for showing such weakness. But this was a small price to pay for freedom. She had to admit the Spider Witch's plan had worked perfectly. The three of them had slipped undetected from the Otherworlds during Tangoo's use—albeit short lived—of the power crystal. It had been enough. They were free, and their enemies were none the wiser.

The Fairimentals now had two crystals in their possession, and soon it would be time for the Dark Sorceress's own plan to begin. She needed only one more crystal in place to begin turning the Fairimental she had chosen to serve her.

The rustle of legs broke her thoughts as the Spider Witch approached.

"Poor thing hasn't had fresh meat for a long time."

The two swept into the castle's dimly lit main chamber, where the witch had already begun work on a new tapestry. Hundreds of spiders hung from the stone ceiling, releasing silken strands of webbing that stretched down to the floor.

"How do you like it so far?" the Spider Witch asked, multifaceted eyes glistening yellow-green within the folds of her hood.

"It has its merits," the Dark Sorceress replied, looking at the patterns already forming on the exquisite strands: trees, rivers, a map of a forested region.

"The blazing star outdid herself," the Spider Witch hissed.

The Dark Sorceress smiled, vampire teeth catching the light. "Your sorcerer made her angry."

"Angry enough to destroy a power crystal. Did you know she had such power?"

"Yes."

"And you still think you can bring her around?"

"Yes."

"I am not so certain, unless, of course . . ." Her words trailed off as she ran her pale, blue-veined fingers along the webbing. In the center, a large, gothic manor house was forming: Ravenswood Manor.

The Dark Sorceress raised an eyebrow.

"The mages must be taught a lesson. It is time for them to learn the meaning of revenge."

Coming Soon!

Avalon Quest for Magic # 3

Ghost Wolf

By Rachel Roberts

This time the battle has come to Ravenswood!

The Dark Sorceress and her evil ally, the Spider Witch, are twisting the magic of Ravenswood and releasing angry spirits of the forests. It's up to the warrior, Adriane, to save the day with the help of her mistwolf, Dreamer and a trusted friend inside the spirit world: Her lost packmate, Stormbringer!

Adriane must walk the warriors path to a whole new level of magic in a fight to the finish!

Available March 2004

KIND News Online

Be a kid in Nature's Defense!
Visit KIND News Online at

www.kindnews.org

The website for kids who care about people, animals and the earth.

Experience even more of the magic:

Become an Avalon Clubhouse member!

To find out more, visit **www.avalonclubhouse.com**

Or write to:
Avalon Clubhouse
P.O. Box 568
Lowell, MA 01853

(Check with your parent or guardian before visiting any website!)